God bless B.J.,

Love, T W Snider

A Dog Named Trash
and
Other Great Stories

SECOND PRINTING

T. W. Snider

A Dog Named Trash
and
Other Great Stories

T. W. Snider

PUBLISHED BY:
BRENTWOOD CHRISTIAN PRESS
4000 BEALLWOOD AVENUE
COLUMBUS, GEORGIA 31904

FOREWORD

My wife, Jan, has worked about as hard as I to get this lovely book out. Thanks Jan. You have carried much of the load.

Thank you, Lisa Stovall, for your hours of efficient work with the manuscript.

Someone has so well said, "Good writing is not written, it is rewritten. Many of these wonderful true stories were harvested years ago. Now I proudly bring them to you. May they bless your heart as they have mine.

Another person who has encouraged my heart to do this, is Dr. E. C. Sheehan. Our warm friendship goes back to the sweet days at Mercer. Thank you, Clinton.

May the message in this book bless the lives of many hungry hearts.

TABLE OF CONTENTS

Mr. and Mrs. Snider

LOVE: WHAT IT IS, WHAT IT AIN'T

Before the minister's meeting was called to order, a young pastor commented, "Love is an emotion." A quietness ensued, and he repeated, "Love is an emotion." An older minister with a doctorate in psychology leaned toward the young man, "Don't ever repeat that again. Love is not an emotion. If love is an emotion, when you get angry with your wife, you don't love her any more."

Emotions are very changeable, Love sticks. "Love suffers long."

Those pastors began trying to define love. The best they could come up with was, "Love is the setting of one's affection." Does this improve the definition any: "Love is the setting of one's affection on a person or a thing?"

"Love not the world, neither the *things* that are in the world." "Set your affection on the things above" (Col. 3:2).

Many people seem to think that a love bug comes flying around like a bumble bee, and when he bites you, you are helpless. Love starts, breaks out like the hives, and you lose all control. You not only have no control, you have no responsibility. The dye is cast.

The truth is opposite. God's Word says, "The spirit of the prophet is subject to the prophet" (I Corinthians 14:32). We are in control of our spirits and love. This is evident by the fact that God commands us to love one another. All through the Bible we are given commands that require such control.

A lady said to me, "I'm going to leave my husband!" I learned that she was going to leave, not only her husband, but her home and house full of children. Enough to make the angels weep! The love bug had bitten her. Or is it better said that the Devil had taken control of her life? He, the Devil, is in the world to ruin people, she had let her heart, her affection, her love and lust go after another.

Her desperate need was to repent of her sins, get a hold of her heart and love, and turn it back to her home, her children and hus-

7

band! WE SET OUR AFFECTION! And God commands us to set it in the right direction. Love is truly the setting of one's affection.

Wisdom and knowledge are very close kin, and properly applied can be most helpful. Knowing what love is, and that it can be controlled, can mean salvation indeed. And it's a mighty step in the right direction. When one's heart has gone astray, he needs to get a mighty hold on his heart, and with the help of God, and by repentance and faith, turn it in the right direction. And the right direction is toward God and God's Son, Jesus Christ!

STRANGE THINGS

Zeno Wall was pastor of First Baptist Church, Shelby, N.C. during World War II. On New Year's Day, in visiting and praying with people whose sons and husbands were in the war, he felt impressed to stop and pray with a family of three children, where the husband and father was away in the war, although they were not his church members. Remember, it was New Year's Day. A strange thing: Six weeks later, a letter came from that husband and father saying that on New Year's Day, they had a war mission to go on. He said that as they sailed toward that war mission, he actually heard Zeno Wall praying for him. That was before the days of television. *What a miracle!*

I had a cancer cut out of my left ear. About two weeks later, upon returning to the doctor, he said, "It's not healing." My wife, Jan had told me this repeatedly. He worked with it and changed the medicine to a much more expensive one. At home with the new medicine, Jan kept telling me that it was still not healing, and I could see the same. I knew a man who had the side of his face eaten off with a cancer. I could just see mine eaten off by that carcinoma cancer.

One night before lying down, I knelt by my bed and prayed earnestly for myself and for healing. In the night, I awoke and was completely wide awake. A spirit appeared to me. All was clear as could be. The spirit looked just like a person, and said,

"Quit using that medicine. Start using alcohol and peroxide, alternately. Then he (it) was gone.

The next morning I cleaned it and obeyed the spirit. Within twelve hours, Jan and I thought we could tell it had started healing. The healing was quick and remarkable.

There are strange things about divine healing. However, everywhere you look in this world, there are strange things. God gave the apostle Paul great power to heal, and that power was on him far greater at times, like on the island of Melita. He could heal others, but he could not heal himself and he said. "Trophimus have I left at Miletum sick."

In answer to prayer, the angels opened the prison door and Simon walked out a free man; yet, Paul the great apostle languished in jail for years. It's ours to pray and trust, and serve God in jail or out of jail, sick or well. Whether we live or die, we are the Lord's

We see through a glass darkly now, but when we arrive in Heaven, the veil will be taken from our eyes, and we'll understand it better by and by. Praise His Holy Name!

SOMEBODY HAS COME AND WE KNOW IT!

If you say you know about Abe Lincoln and his log cabin, or George Washington and his cherry tree, nobody questions it, and nobody doubts it. Yet, the only way we know is history. And we do know!

In the little book of First John in the Bible, next to the last verse in this little book is indeed a great verse: "We know that the Son of God has come..."

How do we know? There are several ways that we know. I mention two or three. One way we know, the same way we know that Honest Abe paid us a visit. History. Years ago, my boyhood friend gave me a lift in a mule-drawn wagon, as I walked home from school. I knew that my friend's dad had sown seeds of doubt in his mind, and I wanted to help him. My history lesson for the next day had a *whole page about Jesus. This was in the public school textbook!*

A mule-drawn wagon, going about three miles per hour, offers time for conversation. So I started reading that page to my friend. He quickly perked up, "Is that in that book?" he asked. I showed it to him. You see, history records the fact that Jesus was here, same as it does that dear old Abe was here. No doubt about it; both those boys walked on God's green earth.

"But we have much more evidence about Lincoln; we have this nation." Yes, and we have much more evidence God and His dear Son have been around here, we have this universe! Then, too, Josephus was a great historian of more than two thousand years past, and he wrote about Jesus, and many other Biblical events.

Then we have the Bible, and it's the best history book in the world. We accept history by faith. There are many other evidences that history is true, so it's not all by faith. And so with the Bible! A witness talks in a court room, and sometimes his words are mighty important.

Romans 8:16 says that God's spirit bears witness with the spirit of every Christian, telling him that he is a child of God. Millions of Christians over the world stand ready to affirm the truth of this, that they have experienced this. This writer is one of them. Our Christian foreparents joyfully and truthfully sang: "He walks with me and He talks with me, and He tells me I am His own...." Yes, Sir: *Somebody has come, and we know it!*

THANK GOD: SOMEBODY HAS COME,
AND WE KNOW IT!

JOB'S WONDERFUL WEALTH
GREATER THAN GOLD

Job, of the Bible, was a rich man. There are dangers in being rich. However, there are dangers in being poor. Solomon was the wisest of men, and he prayed to God, "Give me neither poverty nor riches...lest I be full and deny Thee ...or lest I be poor and steal."

The great danger is not in you and me having riches. It is rather, in riches having us. It is all right for us to have money, just so we are sure that money does not have us. And Job was all right along this line. When his riches were all swept away overnight, he got up the next morning with a song, a little chorus: "The Lord gives and the Lord takes away, blessed be the name of the Lord." For Job was rich in more ways than one. He was rich in faith, faith in God!

I know a man who was raised on a Midwestern farm. One day, his father yelled for the whole family to "Get in the car!" A tornado was coming fast. That old rattling Ford outran that tornado, and they returned to a pile of rubbish. No house. The barn was all right and the stock OK.

"Be careful, don't step on a nail," Dad cautioned as they piled out. Mama was hysterical. Hands high, walking around the car, she kept repeating, "Oh, we've lost everything, we've lost everything!" Finally, Dad grabbed her, "Mama hush! What you are saying is not true! We have not lost everything! We have our lives, our health, our land, one another, and our faith in God!"

That was a rich family, indeed-rich in something better than gold. They took the debris and made a shelter, slept under it and made a crop and harvested it. Every child in that family did well in life. And no wonder with a dad like that.

That's the way Job was, only far more so. And he meant all this and more when he said, "Though He slay me, yet will I trust in Him." He whose faith is fastened to God like that has something better than gold. For this is what ties us to God. It's the ticket through the gates of Pearl and into the city of Gold. AMEN!

STUMBLING BLOCKS, STEPPING STONES

"Whose feet they hurt with fetters, he was laid in iron" (Joseph)

Some folks seem to handle hardships much better than others. There are people who, apparently were born to be overcomers, and can't be stopped. Others, it seems that the wind from the wings of a gnat would blow them away.

Joseph was more than well worthy to rule all Egypt as God's number one man. He had proven this by standing true in some of the worst adversity that anyone ever faced. When it rains, it pours, and it seemed that these storms would never pass. Joseph was indeed a miracle. Left by his brothers to die a torturous death, then sold by them into slavery worse than death. Followed by a life sentence to prison in a strange country. Yet, the worst Joseph had for anyone was, "You meant it for evil, but God meant it for good!"

As an humble slave, he won the trust of his master. But the cards seemed stacked against him and- for being true- he was soon sentenced to prison for life! "Whose feet they hurt with fetters, he laid in iron" (Ps. 105:18). With little or no hope of ever being released, he won the hearts of his fellow prisoners and guards. How his heart must have cried out to God as the years passed! Sometimes we cannot understand God's delays. About half of Joseph's life was spent in slavery and prison. He was both an ideal slave and prisoner. You talk about stumbling blocks and making steppingstones of them—Joseph is our example. Of course, it was God and God's grace. However, God waits to walk with each of us! He will put our feet on the right stones!

Poor Samson was the opposite. God gave him stepping-stones, but he made stumbling blocks of them. His giant strength became a stumbling block and led to imprisonment and death! When on the path to his date with his immoral, double-crossing girlfriend, God let a lion block his path. What a mighty message from the Lord that he was on the wrong path and that he should break up his evil affair. But Samson called on his mighty strength, engaged the king of the beast in battle——and won... and went on his way and to his doom. His strength—the mighty stepping stone, yet it became the death-dealing stumbling block!

Some of us cannot handle even steppingstones, to say nothing of stumbling blocks. Others can go tipping right over the most dangerous stones of stumbling, for these are made into steppingstones.

Jesus is our greatest example in this field, as in many other fields. He is made unto us an example and many examples that we should follow in His steps (I Peter 2:21).

Crucifixion was an awful death. Jesus hung on that cross all day long! In addition to the natural agony of such a cruel death, He had the sins of the whole world upon Him. That means that He had the consequences of sin and that means He had the wrath of God. He took the wrath of God that you and I might enjoy eternally the smile of God (I John 2:2).

Jesus took the most horrible situation that's ever been in this world and made out of it the most glorious thing that can ever be in this world! That cross! It is now, and shall forever be, the "prop" that holds Heaven's door open for the redeemed to walk in! As the songwriter said and as the Bible says in so many places, "There's no other way but this way!"

EARS THAT HEAR, AND TALK

The Wellness Letter of the University Of California at Berkeley informs us that four doctors took it upon themselves to measure the ears of 200 people, ages 30 to 93. Following up on this, they found, sure enough, ears, unlike children, never get grown. They keep on growing. In one year they grew almost none, but in fifty years they grew almost half an inch. Some more than others.

Several scientific studies have revealed that a crease (wrinkle) diagonally in a man's ear lobe is a sign of increased risk of heart disease. Charles de Gaulle and Lyndon Johnson had much in common. Both were leaders of great nations, and both had big ears, and they did not seem to stop growing.

Perhaps our ears and mouths are both talking to us as we grow older. Their messages? Since the mouth does not get larger, we should not talk more, but less, and watch our words. Our ears, by continuing to get larger, are trying to tell us that we should listen more as years go by. For with time ticking away as the years pass, many of us seem to think that we have little time left to pass our storehouses of knowledge to an ignorant generation— that wisdom will surely die with old age. These big growing ears are trying to tell us that we should listen more carefully, and run our tired tongues less.

Jesus warned us that many "having ears hear not" and God, in James tells us big ears and small mouths are just what all of us need, for it says that we should be "swift to hear and slow to speak". We surely need more doctors who specialize in curing diarrhea of the mouth.

There is so much for all of us to see, hear and learn. And so few are longing to listen. No wonder the prophet cried: "HEAR YE, HEAR YE! HEAR AND YOUR SOUL SHAll LIVE!" It's listeners that the world needs, and it's listening that we need. Even as GOD speaks silently to us, if we but listen we can hear His sweet wonderful voice. But we have to stop talking and listen!

GOD LOVES OUR PRAYERS

Did you know that God keeps our prayers, the prayers of His people, in a golden vessel in Heaven? And they are poured out before God from time to time, to God's delight. This means that long after mother is dead and gone, "My mother's prayers have followed me," and it means a whole lot more! And the Book tells us that God delights in the sweet aroma.

Here it is: "The four and twenty elders fell down before the Lamb, having every one of them harps and golden vials full of

14

odors, which are the prayers of the saints" (Rev. 5:8). "And another angel came and stood before the altar, having a golden censer, and there was given unto him much incense, that he should offer it with the prayers of all the saints upon the golden altar before the throne" (Rev. 8:3). This means that our prayers are forever and effective.

It is not written that God keeps our songs or sermons. It is our prayers that God loves so much! Jesus never told us how to sing or how to preach, but He told us how to pray, and gave us a written prayer to guide us. He did not tell us to always sing or always preach, but He told us to forever pray.

Our lord said that praying was and is the way to get things, and the way to get the job done. When Martin Luther was about to be burned at the stake, his friends hid him in an old deserted castle in Germany for a winter or more. Even while hidden away there for the winter he found work to do. He said, "I have so much work to do, I have to pray three hours a day to get it done." There he translated the New Testament into German.

The great man was born to pray, and work, and to be persecuted, and to accomplish mighty things. Jesus said of Paul, "I will show him what great things he must suffer for my name's sake," (Acts 9:16). Some are called to a life of suffering, and all are called to a life of prayer! And what a sweet life it is.

As I look back, some of the sweetest times were times of prayer. Sometimes in a church, some times on the farm behind the plow, even in a horse stable. But always they were sweet times.

SWEET HOUR OF PRAYER!

WHAT KIND OF A MAN IS MAN?

There's something about animals being trained like sheep dogs or blood hounds, trained generation after generation, maybe for hundreds of years – something gets into their genes, their nature. And they become increasingly good at what they are being trained for. It is both their genes and their training. Many of them reach the place where they seem to just live to do that one

15

thing! But you let the training cease and stop them from using their talents and, as the years go by, they will loose much of their attainments. They revert back to the old wild ways.

And you know what? There's something in us like that. Something that draws us away from that which we have worked so hard to attain. At times, even though we try so hard to go upward, we seem to slip back. It pulls us down. And it's forever there! And that seems to be in all realms of our lives.

Our foreparents spoke of that something as the "fallen nature of man." They sometimes called it "total depravity". I hope that by "total depravity," they did not mean as bad or as low as could be, but depraved in every area. You see there's something good and something bad in every person. God must have seen something good in Cain. He put a mark of protection on him that others would not kill him. God did not do that for Satan, for there was nothing good in him, Satan. Cain's heart was pleading to God for help. That was prayer. That alone was good.

WHAT KIND OF A MAN IS MAN?

We strive to go upward and we have to pray and push. But to go downward, we can just turn loose and drift. That something within us will take care of it. Just turn loose and go with the tide and you will wind up in the devil's territory!

Not only does the Bible teach this, thinking men have always noticed it.

Plato lived before Christ. He said: "The cause of corruption is from our parents, so that we never relinquish our evil ways."

Seneca lived back then. He said: "What one blames in another, he finds in his own bosom."

Cicero: "Nature has given us faint sparks of knowledge; we extinguish them by our own immoralities."

Aristotle: "Man is on a slope with his appetites and passions gravitating downward. He knows that he ought to go upward, but there's something in him that drags him downward."

However, the greatest evidence of this is not these men and their testimonies. Rather, it is the clear teachings of the Bible. And above all, it is a cross on the hill called Calvary. *Man crucified his Maker!!!*

However, God took that cross and turned it into the greatest blessing that mankind has ever seen. Look to that cross my brother, my sister, and you can find forgiveness!

HEAVEN

Just the thought of Heaven is glorious beyond compare. What will it really be when we open our eyes and behold, we are actually there! The least we can say will be, "It is the land we have longed for!"

Dying and going to Heaven must be like a great plane going through a very dark cloud, then suddenly bursting through and into the light and landing on a glorious and wonderful shore. Off the plane, we step on the streets of gold. We go through a gate of pearl and there is a table set with a host of our friends of old and loved ones. We are all ready to sit down at the table with Abraham, Isaac and Jacob, just as Jesus said. And Jesus is the light and Lord of it all!

The Bible tells us that there will be great throngs in Heaven from all nations, and tongues and people. Even more than can be numbered — people whose robes have been washed and made white in the blood of the lamb.

Golden streets. I think God is saying that in Heaven they take that which means most to so many on earth, and pave the streets with it in Heaven, walk on it. Some have asked, "Will we know each other in Heaven?" When Moses and Elijah met with Jesus on the mount, Jesus did not introduce them, although they had not known each other on earth. We will know more in Heaven than we do on earth, not less. Now we see through a glass darkly, but then face-to-face, the Bible says.

Some things and some people will not be in Heaven. There will be no unbelievers there. Our foreparents, looking forward, have longingly sung, "No chilling winds nor poisonous breath can reach that healthful shore; sickness and sorrow, pain and death are felt and feared no more!"

Many young and old go to Heaven. And God's children who are seniors, walking on this earth, have felt the dews of the banks of Jordan on their feet. We know that crossing is near, as we brush the banks of Jordan.

One dear old man who had walked with God for many years said, "I got on my old nag to ride off into the sunset. Jesus was with me, and I found that, by his wonderful grace, the sundown of life had turned into the sunrise and the evening into the morning."

John said, "I saw the holy city ….twelve gates … each gate was of a single pearl." No gate was shut by day, and there was no night there. These open gates beckon unto all of us, God's dear children, to look forward with longing to our homecoming. What a homecoming that is for every child of God! Jesus, on the cross, opened the gates and his cross holds them open for us, and they are never closed! (Read Revelation 21, the very back of your Bible).

SATAN'S ADVANTAGE

My friend had two dogs, a Collie and a little dinky dog. After they got rid of the Collie, they kept the road hot carrying the little dog to the Vet. Finally, the Vet said, "If you want this little Buster to be ok, you go get the Collie back." They did and it worked. Such is the power of the mind with both man and beast. Bad emotions can ruin your life, your health, and put you to pushing up daisies.

If I were the Devil, I'd work on people's minds. And that's what he does. When someone does a foolish thing, we say, "Looks like he would have known better than that." Well, in most cases, there was a time when he did know better. But the Devil got in there and twisted the screws around in his head. Satan can really mess up a good mind. It's not a matter of how intelligent he was. Some of the teenagers who took guns to school and killed their classmates at random, and laughed and yelled while shooting them down, were on the honor roll. They had sense all right. When asked why they did it, some replied, "I don't know." That answer could very well be true,

18

for Satan had been turning the screws in their heads. And he's got a screw driver that will fit your head, and my head!

During World War II, the term, "establish a beachhead," became popular. When a beachhead was established, men and supplies could pour in. Well, Satan established a beachhead in those youth's mind, and then he poured out a lot of stuff in. And when that happens, sooner or later, all hell may break loose.

In II Cor. 2:11, in the Bible, we are cautioned to be most careful, "lest Satan get an advantage of us." We have opened the doors for Satan to get an advantage of our country, and especially of our youth. We have invited him to establish beachheads. He gets advantage of us by such as: a lack of honor toward the parents, alcohol parties, hard rock, which at times is about equal to hypnotism.

_A_T_T_I_T_U_D_E_

Just what is attitude? Not many can tell you. Even Webster seems to strain at it.

"Suppose my little Lady, your doll should break its head. Would it help it heal by crying till your eyes and nose were red? Wouldn't it be better to treat it as a joke, and say you are glad that it was dolly, and not your head that broke." Now, that's two different attitudes. All of us are exercising our attitudes all the time.

Attitude? It is an inward disposition, a type of mindset, a way of thinking. And it expresses itself in words and actions. Let me repeat, attitude is an inward disposition, a type of mindset, a way of thinking, and it is forever expressing itself in words and actions.

Dr. Charles Swindell so wisely said; "The longer I live the more I realize the impact of attitude on life. It is more important than facts, education, money, or circumstances. More important than failures, successes of skills. More than what people think, do or say. It will break a church, a company, a home. The remarkable thing about it is, we are in control of our attitude!!!" Thank you, Mr. Swindell.

19

With a bad attitude, one is wrong on the inside, and it scatters gloom and doom all around us. One can get so bitter that he does not like to say that he feels good. One person said that the only time such people are happy is when they are sad.

In Genesis four we have Cain and Abel, the first two who were born into this big world, bringing offerings to God. Abel brought the choice, sweet little lamb. Cain picked up whatever was handy, with little thought or care of pleasing God, God rejected both Cain and his offering.

Now Cain was "very wroth and his countenance fell." After killing his brother, instead of repenting, he pities HIMSELF. This bespeaks his bad attitude. He actually seems to think that he is the one who has been mistreated! Bad attitudes start us on the way to ruin and keeps us there!

But that is not all about attitudes. Habitual, harden criminals are made that way by bad attitudes. Attitudes are in the heart, and control the mind. When your attitude is wrong, you are wrong all over!

And a good helpful attitude is mighty hard to beat! And the biggest step anyone ever made is when the heart turns the feet into the attitude of *love* toward the human race and toward God. And Jesus said that without that, mankind is hopelessly lost: "Except you be converted you shall by no means enter" (Matt. 18:3). When we open our eyes in the morning, we should ask God to help us to have the right attitude toward God and toward all of life. Attitudes of forgiveness open doors for forgiveness coming our way, and going the other way too. We'll be wrong in our opinions many times, but people will overlook much, and God will overlook more, when our attitudes are right!

All night Jacob wrestled with God, in the form of an angel, trying to TAKE the blessing. As day was breaking, his thigh was suddenly out of joint. Now he could only cling to God. With the helpless clinging attitude, he could no longer demand the blessing. Now he could only beg the blessing. And now, as it is written: "And He (God) blessed him there." It is also written:

"And the sun rose upon him." The sun will always rise upon those who have the right attitude.

The right attitude does not simply bring the blessing, it IS the blessing!

MY FRIEND, HAWKINS
THE STORY OF THE CROSS

Some true stories should never be left to die. So, with my dear friend Hawkins. I think it is the most interesting and helpful story that has ever come my way, outside the Bible.

Hawkins and I loved to talk with each other. It seemed that our chemistry jibed. One day he was in a very talkative mood and briefly told me the story of his life.

When Hawkins was a small child, his mother hired a guy to kill his father, paid him thirty cents! Hawkins and his sisters landed in an orphan's home. Two people went to prison.

On Sunday afternoons, people would visit the children in the home and often visitors would take a child home with them. "But nobody ever took me. As the sun sank on Sundays, I'd go behind those big buildings and cry," he said sadly.

Time passed. Hawkins joined the military. On the streets of China, a girl was walking behind her father. He said: "I thought she was the prettiest thing I had ever seen. I followed her."

The two led him to an upstairs apartment and the man got him to lie down on a couch and smoke a pipe. The soldier returned repeatedly, but never did become intimate with the girl. However, he did get something out of it all. He became an opium addict.

One day, on his way to the apartment, he met a guard. As they met, the guard, without looking at him, said: "I wouldn't do it, Hawkins, if I were you." Hawkins said: "I turned and went around the block, and I met him again. And he said the same thing again, without looking at me. I turned again and went back to my bunk."

"The next day I went to see my commander. He asked, "What can I do for you, Hawkins?" I replied, "Sir I am on opium. His chin dropped, as if I had put a bomb under his chair. He exclaimed, "You're on opium?" It was the death penalty then to be on opium in China.

They sent him back to the states. He got off opium. I said to him: "Wasn't it mighty hard to get off opium? I just don't see how you did it. You didn't have any help?" He said "No, not a bit, and it was hard, but I got off it."

Next Hawkins, still a soldier, was in Korea. Let him tell it, "I was lying on my bunk, getting over a drunk. A Christian sergeant stood over me and told me the story of the cross. God imprinted its truth into my heart and the story of the cross – Christ dying for me, even for my sins – lifted me out of liquor, sin, and corruption, and put my feet on the Rock."

Hawkins said: "As a boy, in the children's home, I felt an emptiness in my heart. Seeking to fill the void, I reached my hand and found it filled with opium. But that only bound me. Then in my seeking, I found booze, but it brought more disappointment. This time, I reached and got a hold of the CROSS and by faith and by God's grace, the cross lifted me out of my sin and drunkenness, and placed my feet on The Rock. On Christ, the solid Rock I stand, all other ground is sinking sand!"

Now, with Christ as his Lord, he became a far more useful soldier. Retired from the military he became head chaplain for Ford Motor Company.

My dear friend had a heart ailment. And a few days after charming me with his story he was on a sandy bank fishing. His dear heart fluttered and stopped. And he was in Heaven. That is what the cross was meant for. Jesus said: "And I, if I be lifted up, I will draw all men unto me." Thank God for the drawing power of the cross and for the cleansing and delivering power of the blood.

BROTHER LESTER BUICE, ONE IN A MILLION

One of the first mega churches in the Atlanta area was Rehoboth, and Lester Buice was the pastor as it grew to become such. God blessed him and the church as few churches had ever been blessed.

Late one Saturday night he was called to make a visit to Grady Hospital. Going to his car in the late of the night, in the big parking lot, he was accosted by a tall black man who stuck a gun in Buice's belly and demanded money. The Rev. Buice exclaimed, "Do you know who you are robbing? You're robbing God's man. I'm the pastor of Rehoboth Church." The robber recognized the name, for Brother Buice's daughter had recently been brutally murdered, and both the pastor and church had been much in the news. With the gun barrel pressing hard, the preacher had the presence of mind to say, "What you need is to get saved!" The minister's boldness and this statement seemed to disarm the man, despite the gun.

They began to talk to each other, and a gospel tract took the place of the gun. In the light of the car, the two went over the message of salvation from the tract, point by point. Then and there, they both, got on their knees, bowed their heads in prayer to God, and there was rejoicing in Heaven as a sinner passed from death to life. As this man repented of his life of sin, and as the angels rejoiced, Gabriel found room for another name in God's Book of Life.

The next morning was Sunday. After the sermon, Rev. Buice gave the invitation, all who would receive Jesus, or come for church membership, please come forward. Down the aisle came this would-be robber, extending his hand and heart to the pastor. Brother Buice told the whole story to the church, and never did people rejoice more. What a way to win a person to the Lord Jesus!

Such is the power of our Glorious Gospel! Brother Buice said, "We love for robbers to get saved!"

What a story, what a story! What a Gospel. What a Savior!

By-the-way, this, our dear brother, had only been to the 6th grade in school. But remember, he was one in a million, or a billion. He had much love for God and people, prayer and patience with people, a heart full of the grace of God, and a head full of common sense, plus he was always ready to put his life on the line. And that's what it takes! And that was Lester Buice. Thank God for such a man! He told me this true story! He preached in a revival meeting where I was the pastor, and that's when he told me.

GOD'S LOVE
DOES GOD LOVE ALL THE SAME?

In the Bible, there's no doubt about God's love for everybody. He loves everybody far more than we love anybody. It seems from the teachings of the Bible that God loves the most evil, worthless person far more than we can comprehend. The Bible even says, "God IS love."

In Romans five, we find that when we were ENEMIES TO GOD, God sent His dear Son, and Jesus Christ gave His life and actually died for us. And we were HIS ENEMIES! It's very much like saying that while we were "cussing Him out," He was dying for us! Now, we (the redeemed) are His friends, so He will surely take us to Heaven and He surely loves us abundantly. And He not only loves *us,* He loves everybody!

But does He love us more under some circumstances than otherwise and does He love some of us more than He loves others? I think most would say, "No." And their "No" would be incorrect! I am sure of that. Just one statement from God in the Bible settles that. Here it is: "As it is written, Jacob have I loved, Esau have I hated." (Rom. 9:13). Maybe we can soften that a little: In Genesis 30, we find this: Verse 31, "The Lord saw that Leah was hated" (By Jacob). Well, back in verse 30, we are told that Jacob "Loved Rachel more than he loved Leah". So this means he loved both of them, but loved one more.

You see, that word "hated," as used back then, could mean just plain hated, as *we* now use it. But it could mean, *"loved less."* Now, God did not hate Esau. God loved Esau and promised to bless him and did bless him abundantly. But our sovereign God loved Jacob *more* than He loved Esau. God's word says so!! You can't argue with that. That settles it!

Well, can we get God to love us even more than now? Oh, yes! Just as a son or daughter can get his/her parents to love more. How? By walking obediently, by loving them more, etc.

This is in many places in the Bible. Here is one: Deut. 7:12 "…if you hearken to these judgments (commandments), …the Lord, your God, will love you…" This clearly means God would love them more when they were obedient and loved Him more.

This business of LOVE is a wonderful thing. Remember, we control our love. Let us love God and people, one another. Let us love in our homes and in our churches. Love the children and give time to them. If we love more, we will be loved more. Now abides FAITH, HOPE AND LOVE, and the greatest of these is love.

YOU CAN'T WHIP THE STARS

When God made this great universe and set it in operation, He included certain forces, elements, and laws that affect us daily. By these we win and loose, live and die. As we work and live in harmony with these, we are greatly helped along life's way. If we ignore them, or go against them, sooner or later we are forever broken by them. For instance, the law of sowing and reaping. When we sow our wild oats or our good grain, it brings forth fruit. God does not have to get up and walk across the room and press a button to take care of this. It's a built-in business, and there's no escape. It rewards both our wild oats and our good grain. It is a part of nature, in and all around us.

In talking to a wise friend, I said, "In my long Christian life, I've known a number of guys who got into extra-marital affairs, and refused to repent, or to quit. And to my surprise, several of them had heart attacks and died. Now, I believe that the evil affairs had something to do with the heart attacks." "Oh," he replied quickly, "there's no doubt about it. It puts a greater strain on the heart." See, nature is against you. We need nature as our ally.

Another case I knew. A Mr. Whitehead. He was a high officer in his church, and a wonderful man. But his one weakness was that he just couldn't keep his zipper fastened. Finally, his doctor being unable to help him about his hands and feet giving trouble, posed a question, "Mr. Whitehead, are you a religious man?" "Yes, I am very religious." The second question: "Well, do you live right?" The very honest answer was, "No, I don't." Then the doctor gave the most revealing prescription. He said, "I want you to do one of two things, either start living right or quit worrying about it."

The dear man did neither. Eight years later I talked to him by phone. He said, "My life is no pleasure. I'm walking mostly on what used to be the top of my feet." You can't beat the game of life. Nature has a way of having its way. You can't whip the stars. In the long haul, if not in the short, our chickens come home to roost.

It can be *little* things. My dear friend slept with the wet wind of the night blowing on his naked shoulder. By hurting, the shoulder tried to tell him. Nature talks to us. He listened to its voice. Started keeping it warm and dry, now he is ninety years of age and in the best of health. Nature was meant to bless, not to curse us. *You can't whip the stars.*

There's a strong and revealing Bible verse: "THE STARS IN THEIR COURSES FOUGHT AGAINST SISERA" (Judges 5:20). He was a military general who set himself on the wrong course. In the long haul, when the stars are against you, there's no way to win! You may win many battles, but in the end you will loose the war.

I think that Alexander the Great was the greatest military general the world has ever known, even going beyond Napoleon. When still a young man he had conquered the whole world. And in doing so, he never lost a single battle. Unfortunately, he was not God's man. The stars were not fighting for him. And, can you believe it, he died a drunk at thirty three!

In his winning, he was a looser. The forces of nature stand firm. You will be broken if you go against them. It may be little things, like eating and drinking, or the great eternal decisions. Listening to the voice of nature often is listening to the voice of God. The way to have the stars on your side is to go with the God that made the stars, and that's the God of the Bible. And remember, Jesus is the Bright and Morning Star.

LIFE'S GOLDEN MOMENTS
DAYS WITH DIAMONDS

There are some experiences and moments in life that are most precious, and we tend to take them with us—to hold them to our hearts the rest of our lives. Some of these precious experiences completely change us, they make us anew. Our most precious moments, days with diamonds in them.

The day that each of the disciples first met Jesus, that must have been such a day, a day each could never forget. Then, after hearing Jesus teach and watch Him perform miracles, and feeling His great spirit in their hearts, the time came when Jesus called on each of them for a complete commitment of his whole life to the Lord. And from that day until this day, every one of Christ's true disciples has experienced that high moment. Every child of God can sing, "Oh, happy day that fixed my choice on Thee, my Savior and my God."

In the Bible the experience of that high moment is called "being converted." And Jesus said, "Except you be converted you shall in no wise enter." This is the way we start on the road to Heaven. And you have to start the trip before you can travel it!

Oh, I thank God, and I can never forget that stormy night when my old battered ship saw the light from the lighthouse. And this old ship, that stormy night, somehow or other by God's grace and love came chuckling into the harbor of God's grace and salvation. Of my many years that I have lived, that was the high moment. The second highest moment my life —even eternal

27

love—will be when I see Jesus face to face. That my old ship could begin to sail under His blessed banner was a joyful, life-changing event and moment!

Billy Graham was a teenager, going to school and milking his dad's cows. A tent meeting came to town. After the sermon, the preacher's proposition was: All who get over on Jesus' side, come to the front. Billy hit the sawdust trail. It was a high moment. His life has never been the same.

He had a sweetheart and they were deeply in love. He did the wise thing: went to see her and told her about his new-found faith and Savior. She would have none of his Jesus, his "religion." For hours they talked, and cried——and said goodbye. Billy got into his dad's old Chevy and drove home, blinded by tears. He was both glad and sad. Sad to lose a friend, but glad for the high moment of putting his hand in the hand that hung on Calvary! What a high moment! And a moment that all can experience, and MUST experience if we are to walk the golden streets!

WHO IS GOING TO HEAVEN?

Three young men sat in a log cabin talking, having attended a revival meeting. One of them described the setting of a great temptation, and then concluded: "When you say you are a Christian, you are saying you would not yield to such a temptation."

Was he right? Is a Christian one who has risen above yielding to ANY temptation? One who is never failing, never staggering under any circumstances? In other words, is a Christian one who will never sin again? What do you think?

LISTEN: There are both strong and weak Christians. The strongest are not as strong as Jesus, by far. And we hate to think of how weak the weakest are. Surely, the apostles that followed Jesus were the strongest Christians of New Testament days. And Jesus cautioned them, "Watch and pray, the spirit indeed is willing, but the flesh is weak."

One does not have to be the *strongest* Christian in order to *be* a Christian. A sheep does not have to be the strongest ram in order to be a member of the sheep family. The little weak helpless lamb is a sheep also. Indeed, he is one hundred percent sheep. His strength does not make him a sheep. It is something else that makes him a sheep.

In the Tenth Chapter of John, Jesus told us that He knows every one of His sheep and that He will protect and bring them to Heaven, every one of them. We are also told that Jesus is "Bringing many sons into glory" not part of the way. (Hebrews 2:10)

In fact, we Christians are not going to Heaven because we are strong, or perfect, or anything like that. We are going to Heaven because we are washed, we are forgiven! In the Revelation, there's a mighty statement about those John saw *in Heaven*: "These are they… that have washed their robes and made them white in the blood of the lamb." (Rev. 7:14)

That washing does something to a fellow. It changes him. It puts God on the inside of him. However, it does not make him as good as Jesus. In fact, we Christians *really need* to be changed again. And, believe it or not, God has that second change awaiting us: "Behold, I show you a mystery, we shall not all sleep (die), but we shall all be changed" (I Cor. 15:51). That's talking about when Jesus comes.

It's not perfection that prepares us for Heaven. It is being God's children! Our names are written in Heaven. We have put our hands in the nail-scarred hands! We belong to Jesus! He bought us on the cross. And He will be waiting down by the beautiful gate to welcome us home. And THEN, we will be a whole lot better people.

STRESS! MARY'S METHOD
(AT JESUS' FEET)

These two ladies lived in the same house, had the same brother, same environment and the same visitor. Yet, one is all stressed out, while the other is the epitome of peace! Jesus said: "Mary hath chosen." At least in this case, it was a matter of choice!

John Bunion, in a jail cell for years, from there could write Pilgrim's Progress! Some of the best of the Bible was written by a man sitting in jail; sitting at the Master's feet. You don't have to have the best circumstances to have the best seat!

Marvalla Byah, wife of Senator Birch Byah said, "When I learned that my father, whom I so adored, was an alcoholic and that he was involved in a murder/suicide, the Lord knocked at my heart's door. Then, when the doctors told me I was dying of cancer, the Lord almost knocked the door down. I welcomed Him, and He came in. Now, my Bible, which had been gathering dust, I have found to be wonderful, living book. From its living pages, the Savior has come daily to live afresh in my heart. I have such peace and happiness! The doctor gave me pills for pain and for sleeping. I have taken neither. And I have never slept better, even when I was a child."

Although dying of cancer, she found that Mary's method relieved her of stress and gave her perfect peace!

Beloved, we live in a world of stress. An evil spirit, like a wind of cyclone is sweeping over our world and nation. Let us learn that Mary's method is medicine and cure. Let us come to the Master's feet, for His grace is sufficient, sufficient for the storms of life and sufficient in death!

THAT GRASS-EATING MAN

When Captain Scott O'Grady was shot down in Europe behind enemy lines, he faced both a survival problem and being captured by the enemy. Seems that he began eating ants and whatever else he could find, as taught for survival. But eating ants was awfully slow and not too tasty. Then he noticed the cows as they seemed to enjoy the grass, and were eating it so abundantly, and being sustained so beautifully. So he decided the cowfeed might be better. And grass was so available. Too, grazing among the cows just might help hide him from the enemy.

This hungry and wise man had hit on something. However, he was not the first. Had he and his former instructors known the Bible better, they would not have needed the lesson from the cattle. For king Nebuchadnezzer of Daniel's day was a grass-grazing guy.

In Daniel four is a most interesting story of how this mighty Babylonian king let the things of this world push God out of his life. And, driven from his throne. He was forced to dwell with the wild beasts and eat the grass of the ground with the cattle. For about seven long years this went on. In this new and awful lifestyle, the loneliness, his feeling of rejection by both God and man, was too much for him or any man, more than mind or body can stand.

His hair grew to be like eagle feathers, and his nails resembled their claws. His heart ached for just one friend, but seemingly, no one cared. It is amazing that one so high can fall so far. However, he was a very strong man, and in his darkness there was a slight flicker of a gleam of light. And the dear man kept clinging to it, and trying to move it toward it.

Then a miracle. He said, "I lifted up mine eyes to Heaven." That was the first miracle toward mercy. That a man in his deep darkness would do that. When it rain it pours. Sometimes blessings, sometimes bane. The next miracle: "Mine understanding returned unto me, and I blessed the most high." God gave him back his reason and understanding, his friendship and favor with the people, and his throne!

Our lessons in this are: Lesson one- This sovereign God of Heaven rules in the affairs of men. Vs 17: " that the living may know that the Most High ruleth in the kingdom of men." It is He who puts kings on the thrones and He takes them down. We think we do it, but when the votes are all counted, there's one vote that counts far above all others, and that's the vote of Almighty God."

Lesson two- The place God has, or does not have, in our lives often greatly affects our health, our minds, our duty and destiny. It was when he failed to "break off his sins with righteousness" that he lost throne and his mind.

Lesson three- By the grace and mercies of God, the bird with the broken pinion can fly as high again, and often higher.

PRESIDENTS OF THE GOOD OLD U.S.A.

Of the nine who were not college men, four are consistently listed in the top ten. This is a far greater percentage than the others. We wonder why? It surely must be that these men who had been deprived of much schooling felt that they had two strikes on them. Therefore, felt more strongly the need of applying themselves at their very best . More baseballs are hit on what would be the third strike than either of the other two. They try harder. A wise preacher said: "I have noticed that God blesses effort."

Also, for them to climb the ladder to the presidency with little scholastic training required an abundance of common sense and other precious God—given gifts.

Our 17th president, Andrew Johnson, took office upon the assassination of Lincoln. An amazing thing, which we seldom hear: He had never been to school a day in his life! At five, his father died. At ten, he was working a job. He married Eliza McCordle, and she proved to be a First Lady, indeed, for she taught him to read and to do arithmetic. He was a miracle man and he climbed the ladder: alderman, mayor, congressman, vice president, and then the White House. The south being in shambles, he wanted to help the south much, but Congress stood in his way. He was a great and forgiving man.

Mr. Eisenhower, as a boy, was hospitalized with a bad leg. The doctors wanted to amputate it. The lad was adamant: "No, you are not going to cut my leg off!" He said to his brother, "Edd, if I go to sleep, don't you let those doctors cut my leg off. I want you to help me to pray and God is going to heal my leg." Pray they did, and heal God did. That leg went on many long marches after that and was good till his dying day.

When the great man came to die, he sent for Dr. Billy Graham. He said, "Billy, I want you to tell me again, how to go to Heaven." Mr. Graham told him about repentance and faith in Jesus, and that God forgives in view of the atonement, the death of Christ on Calvary. Of course, the great man listened carefully. Then he replied, "Well, Billy, I am ready to go."

What a great way to go, by the way of the cross! For it is the way of the cross that leads home.

OUR POULTRY FARM

Jan, my wife, can do the strangest things. She ordered a quail hatchery and two little eggs came with it. They both hatched, and that's the way it started in our living room. We stayed up most of the night watching them hatch. One got against a heat bulb and injured his leg permanently, the other died soon after birth.

We then hatched four hen eggs in this outfit, three girls and a boy. Such as this went on until our city-back-yard looked like a country chicken farm sho nuff.

Jan named the rooster Hercules, and that fit him fine, for he grew to be a giant of a rooster. He walked with the greatest of pride as he led his flock of hens in their daily round after bugs and seeds, and who knows what else.

They paid little attention to the fence, except Hercules loved to perch on it for his most proud and victorious crow. So they made their stroll right through the neighbor's yard also. However, this too worked all right, giving the city neighbors a touch of their rural nativity of long ago. Well, let Jan tell her rooster story for herself:

THE RESURRECTED ROOSTER

My rooster, Hercules, is crowing louder, more often, and sounding better than ever. He just celebrated his first birthday, and he is most beautiful. With his buff-colored feathers etched in black, he appears to be wearing a shawl of French lace. When he hatched twelve months ago, I could hold him in my hand, and his buffy-yellow fuz tickled me as he sat starry-eyed looking at the big world.

33

He learned to crow all by himself, never having heard another rooster. Only the instinct given by our Heavenly Father was his teacher. That was all he needed. It was a pitiful try at first, but he never gave up. The neighbors wondered and asked about the strange sound coming from our yard, a one-syllable squak. No one need ask today what the sound is when he crows, and the neighbors love him. He crows at the break of day, he crows at mid morning, at noon, and many times in between. He seems to be making up for lost time, for, in my heart and mind, Hercules is a resurrected rooster.

One morning as he came from his sleeping house to the breakfast place, he had a very obvious problem. Something had happened to one of his strong healthy legs. He no longer walked with his former assurance, but was unsteady, and had to stop and sit before going the whole journey of fifteen feet. He would stand and flap his wings and crow, then, he would sit. Now his days are spent in the small space of the watering and feeding area. He is no longer able to go for his delightful strolls with Snow Flake, Buffy, and Momma Hen.

As time passed and Hercules made no progress in recovering, my tender-hearted husband suggested that Hercules might like to go for an extended restful sleep and no longer suffer with his painful lame leg. So we went to our very good veterinarian friend and he carefully counted out twenty Phenobarbital tablets. With specific instructions we proceeded to administer the lethal dose. The twenty white tablets were dissolved in a small amount of water, and we applied the night-night solution with an eye-water dropper. The process was quick and easy, for the big bird cooperated perfectly. Then he was released to go to sleep on the soft zoysia grass.

My hurting heart did not want him to have to die all alone, so I remained nearby and watched, expecting him to drop over dead any minute. To my surprise, he walked a few steps, stopped and crowed as if the world was waiting to hear him. Then he did a few more steps, flapped his wings, stirring the warm summer air, and crowed again. I was convinced that this was Hercules' last crow!

After waiting about an hour, watching him peck the grass, I left him alone. Later I returned and found he had walked and walked and was sitting under the apple tree. He wanted a better place for his final resting place, I thought. So again I sat and waited, thinking every minute he would give up the ghost. Instead, he decided to walk again, and as the sun sank in the west, he went into an isolated corner of the yard out of sight. I came away feeling sad, but knowing that a good humane deed had been done.

In the morning, my first thought was Hercules, and I thought: We'll bury him in the garden. I wondered just what his hens would think when he did not awaken them with the dawn. Then, as I came from the bedroom to the kitchen, I heard something. It was real. Surely I was awake! It was a crow that sounded just like Hercules! Then again, I heard that all-familiar sound. Wow! I made haste with food to the chicken yard.

There sat Hercules by the feeding trough, waiting for his breakfast! When he saw me coming with the cracked corn, he seemed as happy as I. He stood and gave the most vigorous crow I ever heard. Being a polio victim myself and having a "funny" walk, I have something in common with ole Herk. So I watched him eagerly eat his food and wondered how he could seem to thrive on twenty Phenobarbital tablets, and I vowed never to interfere with his life again.

A LITTLE DAB OF THE GREATNESS OF GOD

Jesus came from Heaven to teach and help us, but mostly to die on the cross for our sins. It was Jesus who informed us that God is so big and greatly powerful that He has even the hairs of our heads all numbered, and that this great God attends the funeral of every sparrow, night and day all over the world. You talk about knowing details, God does!

And He's a God of order and of wonder, and wisdom. We know nothing compared with God. That is another big reason that we should trust Him when the going is rough. God has not promised us that we would be without trials and tribulations. Indeed, He has forewarned us that they would come. He has promised us that in and through His strength and presence we would have strength for the day, and the dark night.

All around us we see and feel the evidences of God, His footprints along the way. Even outside of the Bible we see His precious footprints, and the work of His hands.

He is a God of order, a God of wonder! You betcha!

Morning glories can be most beautiful. I recently took some from my garden, and set them in the front, and a few in the back, of my yard. You know, there are several different kinds, and all are beautiful with blooms of glory, rightly named.

Give them something to "run on" and they will reach for the sky. All that I have noticed, climbing whatever they can get their hands on, wrap around like a boa constrictor. Spending the first twenty seven years of my life in the fields and forest, I observed much of the bewildering beauty of God's creation. Frolicking in the forest and the long days in the fields give a boy a great view of the work of God's hand, and how that it all holds to the magic touch of the hand of its Maker.

For instance, these morning glory vines, like other vines, always wrap around whatever they climb to the right. They never go to the left as they wrap around and climb high to show the beauty of their blooms. Now, how in the world did they learn left from right? And this is true of other vines! All go to the right as they wrap to hold on. Oh, one in fifty may be all mixed up, having lost its equilibrium, and wraps to the left.

They are, in this, like ears of corn, the rows of the grains on the cob are always an even number. Not one in fifty in an uneven number. And even when it is uneven, it's a little scrubby, twisted thing that somehow lost its way. All the good, healthy ones have even numbers of rows of grain. Now, who taught that cornstalk to count? Clearly, it is the handprint of God. It didn't just happen! God puts things *in order*, but man, has messed them up terribly.

Look from the morning glory vine to the inside of us, and there we see God again. The Book says, Blessed are the pure in heart for they shall see God." I used to think that meant that at the end of the journey, when we get to Heaven we'll see God. And doubtless it does mean that. But it means much more. When our hearts are pure, we see God all around us, and even in us.

I never thanked God for the air that I breathed, and for the fact that I could breathe, until I nursed a man dying with emphysema. It took him two years to die. For two years he struggled for one more breath. I decided that the emphysema death is the worse death that a man can die. I learned that, in a figure, our lungs have little hands. We draw the good, fresh air into our lungs and our lungs reach out into that air and grab the life - giving oxygen, and our blood has, in a figure, little red soldiers that float in their boats in the rivers of blood. These little faithful, life-saving soldiers come paddling their boats into our lungs; they say, "Gimme some oxygen." They mix that oxygen with other ingredients which are already in the blood, and it *is our life!*

The Good Book says, "The life of the flesh is in the blood, therefore I've given you the blood to make an atonement for the soul" (Leviticus 17:11).

Those little soldiers (cells) carry that blood, which is our life, to every minute part of the body, even to the toenails!

And the blood will not sustain life until this fresh oxygen is mixed with it. Then it is that it becomes our life! And the Book says that God breathed into Adam THE BREATH OF LIFE, and Adam became a living soul! That breath was from God, and it was the gift of life.

Too many of the men of medical science did not read their Bibles, therefore, they did not understand until relatively recently that life is in the blood. That's why they bled George

Washington to death. They were going to "bleed out the poisonous blood," and they killed the dear man!

Isn't it something that we get our life from the air around us, and the blood within us. God so ordained it. "The life of the flesh is in the blood." And that blood is dead blood until the wonderful oxygen is mixed into it. Therefore, "God breathed into Adam the breath of life, and he became a living soul!" You are mighty right God did. *He* did and *He* did: *God* did and *man* did! The mysteries of life were put in the Bible thousands of years before the most learned men learned them, even though they were before his face.

There are so many mysteries about life, and this is just one of them. Everywhere we look, we see a mystery. And there is an answer to all of them. That answer is a minutely little, but giantly big word. It is: God! He is the answer to the mysteries. Thank God for God! He's bigger and better than all His blessings and greater than all His gifts!

RELIGION OR JESUS

There's a world of difference in turning to religion and repenting of your sins and receiving Jesus Christ as your Lord and Savior.

There's something good about most of the religions of the world. They bespeak man in his darkness and in his quest for God. Buddah was one of the best in this dark field. He had a great truth in teaching that we should think on pleasant things. You would think that he had read the Bible where we are instructed to think on the lovely and pleasant things (Phil. 4). It is good that man searches for God. But, oh how sad that in his darkness, he stumbles deeper into the dark, rather than turning his eyes and heart toward the Sun of Righteousness.

In man's search for God, instead of looking upward, he stumbled into the ditch of darkness, so great is his darkened mind and heart! Romans 1:23 tells us that man in his search, took up worshipping "creeping things." Our own history books tell us that

38

those "creeping things" were DUNG BEETLES! (See Page 7536, in Universal Standard Encyclopedia). Egypt was the world's leading nation back then, and that's the nation that led the world in this dung beetles worship! And it was far more than Egypt, as Romans 1:23 clearly implies.

We, farm boys, saw a lot of the dung beetles. You see, the whole world was our bathroom and these big bugs came immediately and carried part of the stuff away. They made it into balls the size of marbles. Then they stood on their heads and pushed it along, rolling it on the ground to his hole in the ground for his children. WHAT A DIET!

And this is what mankind finally found to worship as HIS GOD!!! These were human beings like you and me! How deep the darkness into which Satan can lead people like you and me is more than amazing! Let us give God the credit: Had not God sent His dear Son into this darkened world and given us the Bible, you and I might be on our knees at the tumble roller's hole, seeking to get a glimpse of our God! How great is God's loving grace in sending His dear Son to pay us a visit and now to give us the Bible as a lamp to our feet! We boys on the farm, used to call these bugs "tumble rollers." So this was the "tumble roller religion."

When a guy says that one religion is about like another, he is in about as deep darkness as those bowing down at the holes. Especially when we remember that such folks think that Christianity is "just another religion." Oh, Lord, have mercy on blind people, the blind leading the blind. All in the ditch or at the tumble roller's hole!

Thank you and may God bless even the tumble-roller worshipers.

GREAT HITTERS, IT'S A HOMER!

A little boy felt mighty big as he and his dad arrived at the baseball park early. He got out on the field with a bat and ball. "Watch me, Daddy. I'm the best hitter in the world!" He threw the ball up, and swung with all his might, and missed it. Two other times the same. He looked at his dad a bit embarrassed. Then, with relief, he exclaimed, "Well, Dad, I didn't know I'm the greatest pitcher too!" That's really making the best of our failures.

When you fail, try again. Success does not depend on our never failing at anything. Babe Ruth, the home run king, was also the champion at strikeouts. So was Hank Aaron, who hit more home runs than the Babe. Although Ruth had him beat percentage wise. Hank batted more times than the Babe. But neither one was a pushover at the plate, despite their many strikeouts.

When they went to bat and the bases were loaded, they had to forget their many strikeouts. They remembered their many home runs, and said, "I'll get another one!"

When you and I are in a crisis, when the cards are down and our backs are to the wall, we must forget our failures. We must remember how many times God has helped us. And we must look to God one more time. God will come through, and He will bring us with Him! "IN ALL THINGS WE ARE MORE THAN CONQUERORS THROUGH HIM THAT LOVED US" (Romans 8:37). Tomorrow, as we look back, standing on Heaven's shore, we'll say, "Why, I was tied in with God. In the long haul I couldn't fail!"

Then too, the Christian life is not exactly the same as a baseball game. God figures in a whole lot more in the Christian life. In it we get on base by repentance toward God and faith in Jesus Christ. Indeed, that's the way we get into the game also. And in heaven, when we kneel at the feet of Jesus, we'll realize better than ever before that we were all on base, by God's grace; and Jesus knocked the greatest home run that even God has ever seen. And He brought us all in! Hurrah for Jesus!

CATS AND DOGS AND KINDNESS

Shadow

America has gone to the dogs – and the cats. These pets have it made in the shade. In my rural American nativitiy, every country family had from one to six dogs, and the cats ran around so you couldn't count them. But they did not sleep in the baby's cradle, nor were they rocked to sleep at night in the rocking chair. Back in those days and out there, a dog was a dog and people were people. Everybody knew there was a difference.

At my home now, our cat is king. It is the law of the Medes and the Persians that nobody speaks unkindly to the cat. He has two servants whom he permits to live in his house, with the understanding that they will open and close doors, stir his food, and always be ready to stop whatever they are doing to serve him. Most times when he eats, one of us must kneel and pat him gently. This makes his food digest better, so he says. And he seems to be a pretty good doctor, for this seemingly works much better than the pills the doctors have us humans take.

I told Jan that I believe she is sticking around close to the kitty so, if the rapture comes suddenly, she can grab him up and take him along with us.

It seems that in many modern American homes the first Bible commandment is to put the dog or the cat first. Instead of the great commandment reading "Honor they father and thy mother," it is now, "Honor thy dog and thy cat, that THEIR days may be most comfortable." Apparently, we have decided that where Paul wrote, "Be ye kind one to another," the "another" means the cat or the dog. After all, he is "another."

With our divorce courts running over, and homes breaking up like straw houses in a storm, it is high time for God's people to rethink and restyle our lifestyles. Surely, it is God's will that we show half as much kindness toward our spouses and families as we do toward our dogs and cats! I guarantee that if we start taking the admonition of Ephesians 4:32 seriously, and start giving one half the kindness that we lavish on our pets, to our families, it will slow the wheels of the divorce courts of the nation and heal most of the hurts of our hearts and homes.

There's nothing to lose and all to gain in doing this, taking God's word seriously. I guarantee it will work! Thank you, and may God bless you. "Be ye kind one to another, tenderhearted, forgiving one another, even as God for Christ's sake hath forgiven you" (Eph. 4:32).

THE ENGLISH LANGUAGE AND THE GOSPEL

I have run into some interesting things in my study of the "English language". English, as taught at Oxford, known as standard English by the so-called "better class" in the south of England, has decreased over the world until it borders on being a dialect. And today, nine tenths of the people who talk English do it the "American way". (More ways than one are used in counting in the language field. Illustration: My friend was born in the little country of Laos, and Laotion was his native tongue. He now speaks English daily, and also his native tongue. Some count only his native tongue. Others count both. In this writing I am counting all who speak any language, i.e., all the students who are studying English over the world).

Four hundred years ago, this tongue was fifth in the world, following French, German, Russian and Spanish. Today it is spoken by more people than French, German and Russian combined, and is required in the schools of many countries, including Germany, Argentina, Turkey and Denmark, and Portugal and Japan. I personally know teachers, natives of the USA, who are now in Communist China teaching English in the public schools!

More than half the world's newspapers, radio and TV stations, are in English, and three fourths the world's mail is in English. How bout that!? I got this about newspapers, TV and radio stations, from the Atlanta Journal and Constitution.

Another language is spoken by more people than English. But these folks live on top of one another, so to speak. They are in piles, while English covers so much of the world, and is spreading so fast. It is already the language of the world, in my thinking.

Listen to this: Before and in New Testament days the Greek language covered much of the then-known world. That's why Paul and the rest of them wrote the New Testament in Greek. God saw to all of this. He had gone ahead and prepared the world for the coming of the gospel. No one language had ever covered so much of the world before. The way was being prepared for the sovereign will of God, and that was for the gospel to go without so many language barriers. God had His world ready.

We live in a day when Satan is working overtime, but God is still on His throne, and He hasn't gone to sleep! He's calling out a people for Himself. Both the Devil and God are making a mighty push to gather in a harvest before this world's sun sinks. We are in the last hours of the evening of the day.

THE GLORIOUS RESURRECTION MORNING
OUR LIVING LORD

In a Texas pastor's office, I said, "G.E., it is rumored out at the school that the head of the department of Christianity does not believe that the body of Jesus arose from the grave." "Well, what does he think arose?" the pastor asked. "I suppose," I answered, "if the rumor is true, he thinks it was a spiritual resurrection."

The pastor stopped what he was doing and looked at me with eyes ablaze, "Let me tell you something! The only part of Jesus that went into that grave was His body! And the part that came out was the part that went in! That's all that went in, and that's what came out! On the cross He dismissed His spirit to His Father, and they took that body down and placed it in the grave. That's all that was in there, and that's what came out!"

All that struck me as a truckload of common sense. Just as two and two make four.

Jesus appeared IN THAT BODY to the disciples. They saw Him, walked with Him, ate with Him. He told them, "Reach hither and feel me." And He was in that body. There could not have been stronger or clearer evidence and proof that this was the same Jesus. They knew Him and they gave their lives for Him! You don't give your life for a hoax!

And another thing: The part of Jesus that will return is the part that went away. He led His disciples outside of Jerusalem to the vicinity of Olivet and Bethany, "and He lifted up His hands and blessed them…" and while He blessed them, He was departed from them and was taken up into Heaven." "And two men stood by them in white clothing, which said, You men of Galilee… this same Jesus shall so come in like manner as you have seen Him go" (See Luke 24 and Acts 1). *ALL of Jesus went away* and *ALL of Jesus is going to come back!* It will be the body that walked the dusty roads of Galilee, taught in the temple, hung on Calvary. The body that was nailed to the tree and bore our sins.

Well did our foreparents sing with joy an anticipation, "I shall know Him, I shall know Him. I shall know my Redeemer, when I reach the other side, by the prints of the nails in His hands!"

A DOG NAMED TRASH

Returning home from working on a cabin on Pine Mountain, fifty miles south, I stopped at a set of trash bins above Warm Springs. As I rolled up I noticed a puppy about four months old at one of the bins, white with a few brown spots, and a badly broken leg. At sight of me he pressed his little body against one of the big bins and shivered. This told me that he had been badly mistreated, for he feared everybody and everything.

My trash disposed of, I proceeded to look him over, and by turning the back of my hand, I was able to approach him and even to pat him on the head. "Old Buddy, you are in a bad fix. Nobody will take you, and there's no food or water here. You will soon die. I don't want you, but my back yard will beat this place; and I just don't have the heart to leave you here to suffer and die."

Had I left him there, I would have left part of my heart. In the front seat, he got as far away from me as possible, but soon he decided that the impossible had happened: he had found a friend in an unfriendly world. As he snuggled close I knew I had a friend that would stick closer than a brother.

Jan, my wife, came out to greet me in the back yard. I opened the door and out he bounced with all three legs, an unkempt sight. "I brought you something," I told her. Then, seeing her disappointment I added, "Maybe I can give him to somebody." To which she added, "I don't think you'll have many callers." The only thing that exceeded his ticks and fleas was both his hunger and thirst.

I named him Trash in memory of his nativity. Two large cats claimed the back yard as their own. Although they had been enemies to one another, they quickly teamed up against this new intruder, which they hated on sight, and despite all my efforts, they beat him repeatedly, with no mercy for his broken leg. The

45

poor pup who seemed born into nothing but hardships surely must have thought this is a horrible world.

He quickly made our little back porch his new home, or at least headquarters, evidently thinking this would be the closest he could get to his new-found friend. His fear of folks and everything else was such that he quickly jumped off the porch every time the door was opened. Loving kindness cured this the very first day, and Trash began to realize he had left the Hell of the past and was now in dog heaven.

All of this took place on Friday. Monday we decided to seek help for Trash's twisted leg. After trying other places, we found ourselves one hundred miles from home at Auburn University Animal Clinic, Auburn, Alabama. I learned they had twenty animal doctors, some of them specialist. This assured us that we had brought our treasured broken patient to the proper hospital. It cost $500.00. A vet told me she would have charged $1,000.00. It was not an out-patient job. We left him several days.

We found the Auburn hospital to be highly efficient. Trash was assigned to one particular senior student so he would get the best of care. And this student called us each night, collect, to keep us completely updated on the welfare and progress of the patient. He informed us that Trash had become very famous at Auburn. Evidently his new-found fame was due both to his name and his nativity, the trash pile. It seemed that it was news indeed that anyone would pick up a pup from the dump and pay a big hospital bill out of love for a dump dog named Trash.

The broke leg and pelvic being old, healing was slow, but complete. Trash grew to be about fifty-five pounds, and turned out to be mostly Pit Bull, and was always superior to his name. He was not vicious, but he could never forget the beatings those cats gave him when his leg was broken, and he vowed war on all cats till his dying day, especially those two. He often dared them enter his yard. I tried to intercede and be a peacemaker, but to no avail. I'd say, "Trash, don't be mean, be good to the cats." He would look at me with those big bull-dog eyes, and the message was, "Huh, why didn't they be good to me when my leg was bro-

46

ken!? I ain't forgetting and I ain't forgiving!" (This writer is a Baptist) I looked back at Trash and said, "Trash, you are a revelation! I believe you are a Baptist! Forgiveness is not your specialty."

"Me and Trash" became big buddies. On Pine Mountain he could roam the woods by day and lie by my bed and by the fireplace on cold nights. I kept the fire going all night in cold weather. Yes, for Trash, but it also felt good to me too, especially getting up on cold mornings. Here at home south of Riverdale, we often walked around the block, and he got to meet many other dogs. Really, dogs larger than he, he would stand over them, if I permitted, and he'd growl. Then he'd back off and say, "Now, don't forget who's boss." Really, they seemed to understand that Trash was Pit Bull.

Never did a dog love his master more than Trash loved me. If I was gone for a couple of days, if possible he would find one of my socks and lie on it until I returned. And, as said, he could talk to me with those big Bull-dog eyes. One day I said, "Trash, you ain't no good. You are just an old dump dog. I ought to take you back to the dump!" Those eyes would talk to me: "Oh my master, don't talk like that. You are the only friend I ever had. At that other house they were mean to me. They broke my leg. Then they took me to the dump and left me to die. You got me. Got the fleas off, and took me to the doctor. You fed me and gave me water. Oh, my Master, I love you. Just let me lie at your feet!"

Another reason I loved Trash: He reminded me of myself. We had so much in common, despite that he was a dog and I was a guy. Once in my life I was at the Devil's dump, full of ticks and fleas from the Devil. Our sovereign God came along. He looked me over. Then He said, "T.W., don't you want to go with me?" I was overwhelmed and asked: "Dear God, would you let me?" His eyes were full of love as He answered kindly, "Yes, I'll be glad to have you! In fact, I've waited for you a long time."

He took me in His arms of grace and placed me in his invisible chariot. Took me to Dr. Jesus who got the ticks and fleas, and some other things much worse, off, by washing me in His precious life's blood.

47

Now, after all these years, God is still my best friend. He's in the business of finding people at the Devil's dumps. God is our friend, He's not our enemy.

GRANDPA'S CLOCK

The old-timey grandfather's clock on the mantle had a heap-o works in its belly. Little wheels, hairspring, mainspring, pendulum, on and on. And it seems that every one of these little trickets was vitally important.

Long ago, I heard a teacher say that we choose what we believe. The more I have thought about that, the more I believe it is true. It really is true. We choose what we believe. About the clock, I choose to believe that it had a maker, that it did not make itself. If I were allowed to say that I believe that clock made itself — well, I think you'd be ready to send me off.

Now, you believe whatever you want to believe about the clock and I'll do the same, and we will still be friends. We won't "get mad" toward one another 'bout that.

Well, the same thing about the universe. You choose your belief and I have chosen mind. THE UNIVERSE IS A MILLION TIMES MORE COMPLICATED THAN THAT CLOCK. But if you choose to believe that it made itself and that all of life in this world was once a little gob of mud — then one day it moved a wee bit, then a bit more. Lo and behold, all came from that little gob of mud! Now, you can teach that in all our schools and I'll put up with it without getting angry with you. I'll still love you.

On the other hand, I trust that you will be kind enough to permit me to express my belief and you will hold your temper. That gob of mud — where did the mud come from? And the Big Bang idea — that there was once a mighty explosion and when the dust cleared, heaven and earth were in their places with all the trimmings and all was operating perfectly! That reminds me of the guy who believed that the first Webster's dictionary came about as result of an explosion in a printing shop. It also reminds me of a verse of Scripture: "Their foolish hearts were darkened; professing themselves to be wise, they became fools (Romans 1:22).

We Bible believers believe that "God breathed into Adam and the breath of life and he became a living soul. Then Satan grabbed us up and went running off with us and on the cross Jesus bought us back. The Word says, "You are bought with a price". (I Cor. 6:20 and 7:23). We are God's children from the hand and heart of God! Yes, Sir, the clock had a maker, and so did the human race!

Yes, Sir, again. We believers belong to God in a double manner. One: He made us. Two: He redeemed us. On the cross, He bought and brought us back!

THE SON OF A HARLOT

It pleases God to pick people up out of the Devil's trash pile and let the world see just what God can an does make out of them. And this writer gives thanks for being rescued from the burning in that pile. God delights in bringing beauty out of ashes. Jephthah was whipped to start with. Our psychologists would not have given him a dog's chance. His dad was an adulterer, and he had a harlot for his mother. As if this was not enough, he was a homeless street lad (Judges 11:1 —).

One day Mama said to Papa, "Our boy does not need to be raised on the streets. He needs a home. I assure you that you are his Pa. Would you see what you can do about it?" Although Papa had stepped out of the narrow way, he was not all bad. His answer was, "I not only will see, I'll take him into my home!"

He went beyond that, he took the dear lad into his heart also. For the first time little Jephthah lay down at night with his head on a pillow of security. It was a good home of love.

But Satan seemed to have it in for that boy, and as the years rolled by, the love and goodness took wings and went away. Some half brothers were born. They grew and learned Jephthah's secret: He was the son of a harlot. They hated him! And they made it so rough for our hero that he could take it no longer. Home had become hell!

With no place to go, Jephthah went. However, when the days were darkest, his dad had taught him which way to turn. Judges 11:11, informs us that Epithet "uttered all his words to the Lord". Jephthah "bucked up against it." He was not a "give upper!" With all odds against him, before it was all over he made good! God's people are not "give uppers." We are "more than conquerors through Him that loved us!"

Remember, when the world would get you down, we are not of Him who turns back, the good Book says. Our Lord stuck with it until He could say "IT IS FINISHED!"

Then, back home, things were going bad for the half brothers and their neighbors. A strong army was headed for them, and they had no leader. They remembered Jephthah, and they came begging: "Would you come and be our leader?" He said, "Why, I was with you and you ran me off!" They begged. "Alright, I'll come." Come he did and win they did! Jephthah became King over all Israel! Not bad for a boy who was born a bastard, and raised on the streets, Dear Jephthah climbs to the top. Don't tell me that the son of a harlot can't make good. Put your hand in the hand that hung on Calvary and you've already made good!!!

THE WOMAN AT THE WELL

In John 4, we have the story of Jesus and the woman at the well, a Samaritan woman. The racial tension between the Jews and the Samaritans was the worst in the world and believe you me, that was bad. Races have always hated each other and will until Jesus comes. The Devil will see to that. The Jews would travel far to avoid going through Samaria, but Jesus "must needs go through Samaria." This was for two reasons: To help this woman, and to teach us lessons.

Besides being a despised Samaritan, this woman was a bad gal. Evidently, she had been married five times and now is living in adultery by shacking up. You see, shacking up did not begin yesterday and it's just as sinful now as it was back then.

Most religious people would not be standing in the line to meet this lady. But, Jesus walked miles to meet her and He awaits her on the well. With Jesus, everybody is somebody!

It is true that she had been married five times, and is now living in adultery. If there's any one thing that is clear in the Bible above other things, it is that God loves sinners. Jesus said, "The Son of Man is come, not to call righteous, but sinners to repentance." Therefore, He seeks this evil gal.

The next thing that shines so clearly in the Bible is that God uses sinners saved by God's wonderful grace, no matter what their backgrounds may be. All of us have bad backgrounds. Our sins nailed the Son of God to the tree! How could we have done worse than that!?

"Go, call your husband," Jesus told her. "I have no husband," was her reply. Now listen to what He said: "YOU HAVE ANSWERED CORRECTLY IN SAYING YOU HAVE NO HUSBAND. YOU HAVE HAD FIVE." Because she has been married to five does not mean she is now married to any, to say nothing of five. However, she is a lost sinner. No more lost than if she hadn't been married to five.

Every lost person is one hundred percent lost, and every saved person is one hundred percent saved. If you die right now, you go to the one of the two places and you go one hundred percent. Jesus does not half save anybody. It's ONE place, ONE way and a one-way ticket! And Jesus said, "I am the way, the truth and the life, no man cometh to the Father but by ME" (John 14:6). In verse 26, Jesus told this fortunate women that He, Jesus, was and is the Christ. She believed Him, and that was the turning point of her life.

Now, is the time to do what ought to be done.

SINGING IN THE SHADOWS
THE RAINBOW ON THE DARK CLOUDS

I was moved by a large news picture of a dear woman in Africa who had been driven from her home by evil men. The government of her country had changed over and she could not return home. At the same time, the country where she was currently, would not let her stay. So she was in some pickle! She was indeed homeless. With her hands lifted to Heaven and tears running down her cheeks, she cried, "My home is in the skies!" Such is only a drop in the ocean of the troubles in this world of weal and woe. It seems that Satan and his forces are on a rampage, knowing that they don't have much longer.

However, I have noticed that the country where Jesus lived when He made His trip from Glory to Galilee was by no means without trouble. His country was overrun by a foreign government. Tax collectors for this hated government used force to collect unjustly. Poverty abounded with homeless beggars in the streets. Much disease and sickness, even leprosy, and not a single hospital in the whole country.

Jesus did not live in a paradise while on earth. Lepers were just driven from home, and not even permitted on the streets close to other people. Mental patients actually lived in caves, or wherever they could. And listen to this: God had given to His people instructions for a way of life, but religious leaders took it and so warped and twisted it, that it had become, Jesus said, "A burden, grievous to be born." Indeed, the sins of the people had dried up the flow of milk and honey to God's Promised Land.

Despite all this, and much more, Jesus seemed to be often smiling and singing a glad song. The Bible says that God had "anointed Him with the oil of gladness above his fellows" (See Psalms 45:7).

Sharing His attitude and glad song is the privilege of His followers. And it roots in and grows out of our faith in God. By means of this faith, we have a new life, a new companion, Jesus, and a new home in Heaven. This puts a spring in our steps and a song in our hearts. All this, an much more, gives us a song as we walk the shining way from earth to Glory.

While our Lord was anointed with the oil of gladness, He was not oblivious to the loads of sufferings all around Him. Indeed, He was also a man of sorrows, and He bore our griefs. Because this world is so filled with suffering, He taught us to pray, "Thy kingdom come, thy will be done, on earth as it is in Heaven." This prayer will be answered. Then the lion and the lamb shall lie together, and a little child shall lead them. And the knowledge of the Lord shall cover the earth as water covers the sea.

(See Isa. 11 and 65:25)

SMILE, BOYS, THAT'S THE STYLE
WHAT'S THE USE OF WORRYING,
IT NEVER WAS WORTH WHILE.

The late Norman Cousin was editor of the Saturday Evening Review, and his name is well known among doctors. He was diagnosed by the best specialists as having an incurable disease. The candid doctors told him there was no hope, and that nothing awaited him on this earth but suffering and death.

He said within himself, "These doctors say I am going to die, so there is no use for me to go their route, for they themselves say it leads to death!"

He was wise, he got the good doctors to agree to help him, and to let him be the boss. The first thing he did, he said, "Lying in this hospital, listening to grief and groans, watching people die and be carried out, is not a place for a sick person." So, with the doctors agreement and help, he got himself moved to a hotel suite.

Then he got many lively, funny tapes to hear and watch, and he laughed a lot. The whole crew managed to keep a jolly good spirit with many happy hearts. And the patient with the incurable disease began to get better! Hallelujah! He actually sang and laughed himself from the door of death to the mountain peak of good health! Got well, and afterwards taught in one of California's universities for years.

This should not surprise us. It is in harmony with the Bible: "A merry heart does good like a medicine, but a broken spirit drieth up the bones" (Proverbs 17:22). This tells us that medicine is a good thing, and that joy and gladness is equally good. The Good Book says, "Singing and making melody in your heart to the Lord" (Eph. 5:19). In Philippians 4, helpful, pleasant things are named, and we are told, "Think on these things, and the God of peace shall be with you." And God speaks again: "Keep your heart with all diligence, for out of it are the issues of life."

We Christians have something to sing about, as we walk with Him who is the light and joy of Heaven, for we are on our way home, and we can continue our eternal song when we get there!

PASS THE PEAS, PLEASE

America is headed for the ditch, or is already there morally. Not the least of the many contributions towards this is the absence of helpful family life.

In the bygone days, family lifestyles tied them together and strengthened the young for the battles of life. Back then, compared with now, children encountered almost nothing that pushed them toward immorality and evil. Now, that is about all many do encounter.

Back then we were rural. Now, we've followed Rome to the cities. And we are on her trail in many other ways, including the path to ruin.

In old time country life, mealtime was a gathering of the whole family around the table. Even three times a day they thus gathered to enjoy the fruits of hard-working hands. Even the aroma from the food was such that it would have awakened a bear from his winter slumber. Mama was home and she saw to that.

There's something about the whole family eating together, makes home, home and gives them a feeling of security and belonging. So reported the American Psychological Association in their recent meeting. More than 500 teenagers were tested

about family relations. It was found that where families
together, the old-fashioned country style, the children we
blessed throughout life from it. They were:

1. Better Adjusted
2. Less likely to use drugs
3. Suffered less depression
4. Did better in school

This writer could have told them that. Some of the sweetest
memories of my life are those of my boyhood around the table
with the whole family.

My comments are:

1. That's the way to raise children.
2. Make mealtime happy, not a time of correcting the children.
3. Bow your heads and give thanks to God before eating.
4. Jesus often ate with His disciples.
5. The Jewish people had many feast days, ordered of the Lord.
6. Yes, the table can tie the family together for life.
   Encourage it.
7. PASS THE PEAS, PLEASE.

T.W. Snider in his garden.

55

LONELINESS
TO THE MILLIONS OF LONELY PEOPLE

a farmers' newspaper surprised me. These fel-
...us leave them and they live alone, far more than the
average in America, and that's a heap. Perhaps these ladies long
for the bright lights and tire of loneliness. How different from the
souls of the soil of yesteryear! When these men of the past, the
backbone of our nation, came in from the fields, they had three
great blessings awaiting them: A pair of loving arms and a delicious meal. How different from a cold house!

My dear friend was a farmer. He and his wife had sixteen
children. When the youngest became a teenager, all the others
had "flew the coop." Then one day mama and the last teenage
daughter packed their duds, and with hats in hands, they hit the
road, never to return!

The house was at the end of the road which came winding
like a blacksnake through the cotton and corn fields, and was
almost on the banks of the Ogeechee River. A perfect place for
loneliness. After living alone for months, my friend said to his
son, "Allen, loneliness can kill you." He had tons of it. No one
had a bigger dose, or was better qualified to tell us.

But you don't have to live at the end of the road to be lonely.
Our cities are drowning in that stuff. Someone said, "There's
enough loneliness in one city to lonely the whole world."

Scientific studies reveal that my friend was right. This heart-
hurting plagues is dangerous and can kill. Is there a pill for this
purpose? Is there balm in Gilead? Yes, there's balm in Gilead.

THE ANSWER: TWO SMALL STEPS, ONE BIG ONE:

1. Purpose. Get up in the morning with purpose for the day,
in big and little things, and *get at it!*

2. Start helping people. Briefly visit someone, maybe a nurs-
ing home. Others are hurting too. This is important.

3. Last but not least, GET RIGHT WITH GOD! Apologize to
Him for ignoring Him so much and so long. Pray to God three
times a day as Daniel did. You'll be surprised at the good God

will do you. With God's help you can whip loneliness, and all else that is against you.

The apostle Paul of the Bible stayed in jail for years. So did Joseph. Yet we do not hear these great men crying out about loneliness. They had found the answer. The answer is GOD.

God is the pot of gold, and He is not at the end of the rainbow. He's nearer than hands and feet, and closer than the breath we breathe. For in Him we live and move and have our beings. God is what you need. It is not religion. It is the God and father of our Lord Jesus Christ. You will find Him when you kneel before Him, repent of being a sinner, and open your heart in love to Him.

OUR THORNS AND BITTER WATERS

Tom Dorsey was a Black man who wrote a great song. His wife and child had both died and were put in the same grave. From his hurting heart, here is the song: "Precious Lord, take my hand, lead me on, let me stand. I am tired, I am weak, I am worn. Through the storm, through the night, lead me on to the light. Take my hand, precious Lord, lead me home."

God's children often wonder why we encounter so many dark valleys and raging storms. And no wonder! As we move deeper into the last days of this age — the "time of the end," as it is called in Daniel 12:4, Satan is working and raging most ferociously, for he knows that he has only a short time. Never have there been days like these. However, hardships often bless us. They make us or they break us.

Paul really wanted his "thorn in the flesh" removed. But God said "No" and He stuck with his "No." Eventually, Paul rejoiced about his trouble. He found that God could, and did, turn his weakness into strength, his bane into blessing. Paul said, "Therefore will I glory in my weakness (afflictions) that the power of Christ may rest upon me (See II Cor. 12:7).

Joseph never spoke greater wisdom than when he said to his brothers, "You meant it for evil, but God meant it for good." That was his gracious way of saying to his brothers, "Don't let it worry you." The lessons of the bitter waters of Marah are hard to beat. Picture Moses with more than a million people, children and cattle in the burning hell of the desert. Overwhelmed with thirst, they are coming to fresh water. They will soon die without water. Bitter here means poison, and that's what this water is. But the bad turns out to be the good. God directs Moses. He cuts a certain tree and casts it into the water. Lo and behold! The bitter becomes sweet! Death becomes life!

God had led them and they had followed, and here is the awful poison water directly in their path, the path that God has led them. They cried to Moses, and Moses cried to God. Sometimes we need a shoulder to cry on, and you can't beat the shoulder Divine!

The cure for the poison water was a certain tree, and that same tree is *our* medicine and cure, after the Son of God has been nailed onto it, it is the cross! It has a wonderful way of turning all our trials into treasures. For God's child, sorrows are plentiful. His school is in the valley of affliction. Jesus is the Principal. He's a Man of Sorrows. However, to our delight and need, this Man of Sorrows has now been anointed with the oil of gladness (Ps. 45:7). Therefore, we can now come with all boldness to the throne of Grace. Now we linger not at Marah with its bitter waters, but on the Elim with the shades of its pleasant palm trees.

ON OUR KNEES WE STAND TALL

Let Him That Thinketh He standeth Take Heed Lest He Fall

While our paychologists are trying to get us to think more highly of ourselves, God, in His word, is trying to get us to think more lowly of ourselves. The apostle Paul wrote, under Divine inspiration, "For I say unto every man that is among you not to think more highly of himself than he ought to think" (Romans 12:3). The world around us would have us think big of ourselves and little of God. That is the tallest mountain peak of error and the lowest pit of depravity. And the Bible tells us the opposite: That man is a sinner and has lost his way! And that the only way that man can ever amount to anything before God and stop his downward slide, is to come crawling back to God in the dust of repentance. Thus God will receive him, forgive him, exalt him.

Jesus said, "Whosoever exalteth himself shall be abased, and he that humbleth himself shall be exalted" (Luke 14:11).

Jesus Christ humbled Himself. He was head of all Heaven, yet He left it for the pain and agony of the cross! He became, not a King on a throne, but a servant, and even a criminal on the cross, for He took our crimes. Even willingly became an outcast, homeless, street person, for He said, "The Son of Man hath not where to lay His head." And He taught us, "If any man will be great, let him be the servant of all." And He told us, "The first shall be last and the last first" (in Heaven).

When we bow ourselves into the dust of the earth, repenting of our sins and unworthiness, then it is that the God of the universe stretches out His loving arms to us, and makes us to be His very own! Then it is that we become heirs of God and joint heirs with Jesus Christ! Even Kings and Priest unto God.

Indeed, we have something to brag about. We can walk right to God on His throne and talk to Him! We are sure and assured that He has a home in Heaven awaiting us!

Not only all this, He condescends and walks and talks with us, and assures us He will never leave us.

And all of this is because of Jesus Christ. He went to Calvary and put away our sins, washed us whiter than snow! When we hear our heels popping on the golden streets, we'll know that we are something alright, and made that way by Jesus Christ. Thank you, God, for loving us and giving to us yourself in the person of your dear Son! JUST AS THE BIBLE SAYS!

EYES THAT SEE

Years ago, when segregation was the law of the land, I dropped into a Black church one week night, deep down in Dixie, to hear a good sermon. It was in my rural native country side, and the speaker was from the city. The sermon was far from a disappointment. The Black man fed our hungry souls. Although it has been much more than 60 years, I well remember his subject and text: "Blessed are the pure in heart for they shall see God!" And his sermon has stayed with me, for God implanted it into my soul.

I had always thought that meant, one day, in Heaven, if our hearts are pure, we shall see God. But my good brother did not see it that way at all. He said, "Up in Atlanta, a man fell from a tall building. He was hardly hurt. They said, It's a miracle! They saw a miracle! I saw God! As I came down from Atlanta, the farmers' crops were a wonder to behold. The rains had come. The sunshine had blessed them – the cotton, the corn, the gardens. Some folks, he said, "saw only nature. I saw God in the growing of the crops."

It was clear that my brother had better eyes than most of us. Jesus said, "Having eyes, they see not." He also said, "Blessed are the pure in heart, for *they shall see God*." This dear man's heart being right with God, had opened his eyes to a new world.

Elisha, of the Bible, and his servant went to Dothan. The servant arose early in the morning. Lo and behold! As he looked out, he saw the city was surrounded by their enemies. He exclaimed, "O Master, what are we going to do?" Elisha answered, "Don't worry, Son. They that are for us are more than they that are against us!" Elisha prayed that God would open the eyes of the lad, and God did. The servant saw the mountain was full of horses and chariots of fire! They that are for us are more than they that are against us!

David, the Psalmist, looked at the stars, and they talked to him about God. "The heavens declare the glory of God, and they show the work of His hands." What you see in the stars depends on what's in your heart!

Ever since Adam, God has been reminding us of His love and kindness. The Bible says, quote, "He left not Himself without witness, giving us rain from heaven and *fruitful* seasons, filling our hearts with food and gladness." It was God who fixed the tree to give us fruit as a reminder that He cares for us!

Let us never be like the hog under the acorn tree. Never looking up to where they are falling from. Every time you pick the fruit from the tree, it is saying to you, "God put me here, just for you." The heart of God talks to us mostly through His Bible, His Son and His Great Spirit. And His greatest message to us is the message of the cross on which Jesus died for our sins, and was resurrected, our living Savior. For herein we have the forgiveness of sins and everlasting life.

WHY DOES GOD LOVE US?
THE BIG REASON

God's great love for us is PRIMARILY because of what is IN HIM, not because of what is in us. Let me illustrate. Among the many great mothers since Mary, the virgin mother of Jesus, John Wesley's mother, Susannah, towers like a mighty mountain. Had England been pushing abortion back then, as now in America with the blind leading the blind, and had Susannah not been God's choice mother, we would not have John nor the Methodist Church. For John was the fifteenth of her nineteen children. She schooled them magnificently at home, and even taught then to "cry softly" when they must cry.

An illustration of her efficiency is well seen when one night she awoke to find the whole house engulfed in flames. Instead of bedlam, confusion and despair, she quickly had all of them outside, but a head count found only eighteen! "Look, Mama, there's John!" The little six-year-olds face was framed in an upstairs window! Quickly she had one man on another man's shoulders rescuing her precious boy. Just as John's feet hit the ground, the roof fell in. He always said, "I am a brand from the burning!"

Despite the wonder of her work, we feel sure she was not rolling out the red carpet when she learned that John the Fifteenth was on his way, to say nothing of the nineteenth. Some of us would have classed that last as a squalling little red-faced brat, under those circumstances. However, Susannah loved him none the less. The beauty was in the eye of the beholder, and this great mother could not have loved him more. This overwhelming love was not because of what was IN HIM, but because of what was IN HER!

Some of the most beautiful babies have been found in trash cans because the "so-called mother" did not have in her what Susannah had, not in her arms, but in her heart. The right kind of a mother loves because of what is IN HER, and you may be sure that our God is the right kind of a God!

This writer was blessed equal to John by a mother's love. Had that love been because of what was in me, it would have been weak and changeable. But since it rooted in her heart, it was unfailing and abiding, for now abides faith, hope and love, and the greatest of these is love. Paul spoke a mouthful when he said "He loved me and gave Himself for me" (Galatians 2:20).

AFTER THE DARK NIGHT, THE SUN RISES
JOB SAID, "HE THAT'S BORN OF WOMAN IS FEW DAYS AND FULL OF TROUBLE."

When our two little quail were hatching, we stayed up all night and watched and listened to them. It was schooling indeed to us. The book told us when they would hatch, and sure enough, right on time, just like the rising of the sun. First, we could hear a little peep, then the egg would move. Then we could hear the little unborn guy pecking. Really, they peck their way out. With their feet up close to their heads, they peck and kick. As they do this, the egg shell turns, or they turn in the shell, and peck a straight line all the way around. Then the shell just falls apart and they are free, strong and robust in their new world. The first had an awful and long battle before he came out jumping with joy in his new world. It took almost all night for him to work his way out of that prison, and he stopped many times to rest.

The second one seemed to be having an even harder struggle, and finally we decided to help him. So with the eyebrow tweezers we did, and we were proud of ourselves and of him. We pulled off little bits of shell, and right out he came. We said, "Gee! We saved you a lot of work, ole buddy." And you know what? In three minutes he was dead! See. THEY HAVE TO HAVE THOSE STRUGGLES. You don't relieve everything of all its struggles and hurts. And that goes for rearing children. Struggles make us strong.

Everything has to have its struggles. It is the struggles that strengthens all the organs of their little bodies and prepares them for the fights that await them. A wise doctor said, "It takes energy to make energy." It takes struggles to be able to struggle. Even of Jesus it is said, "Though He were a son, yet learned He obedience by the things which He suffered" (Hebrews 5:8). The good Lord's school for His children is the University of Affliction, and it is located in the Valley of Sorrows.

When Jan, my wife, was little, polio got her at the age of six months, messing up both legs, especially the right one, and the spine and right foot. The doctors said she would never walk, for she had no walking muscles left. However, children often do not know what they can't do, so they go right on and do it. She learned to balance herself from the waist up, lock both knees, and make a few steps, without walking muscles, as if on stilts. Doctors have told her that they have never known that before. Now, all together, she has walked thousands of miles that way. However, this becomes much more difficult as the years pass, especially since now she has post-polio syndrome. This last seems to me to be that the overused muscles are now giving out.

They were living on a farm in Alabama near both the Georgia and Florida lines. All farm families were poor back then, for it was the Great Depression days. The mother said, "This child can't go to school if we don't get something done." Far-away Mobile was the nearest place. Since they did not have the money to go with her, and had other children and much work to do, they packed a card-board box for her suitcase and headed for the Greyhound station in Dothan. As that bus pulled off, they waved goodbye, then cried all the way home. But the little girl was thinking about all the ice cream she was going to get. For her father had told her, "They'll have all the ice cream you can eat..." and on and on.

Well, it did not turn out to be exactly an ice-cream party. Rather it was pain and lonely days and nights, and even stretched into fifteen trips, covering a period of many years. Mostly in the summers while school was out and most of the summers all the way through. All of these fifteen trips were made alone except one, and never a single visitor, not one.

The villain polio had turned the top of the foot to the bottom, and she walked on what was supposed to be the top, if you could call that scrambling along walking. Those doctors were far behind medical science and doctors of today. Their procedure was too horrible to tell. To turn the foot over they did not give her even an aspirin. Just put her on the table, and while strong arms held her, a doctor took that little shriveled, distorted foot, and with main force, broke the ankle and turned it over. It was like taking your elbow or knee and bending it completely backward from its regular bending position, and of course breaking it severely. However, somehow the poor child survived the awful ordeal and it finally healed. At least they got the job done.

With braces, she could hobble, and even go to school. But she hated those braces, for she saw that other children did not wear such. Finally, she went out to the corn crib on their farm and threw those braces as far as she could up over the corn, and said, "Good riddance!" The next morning she strapped those places good and tight and went to school. And not only went to school, she became a cheerleader, and learned to do a flip at the football games, and became Miss Headland High School Queen. Not bad for the handicapped who had trod such rough roads.

64

Listen: I have noticed that this lady has more compassion for hurting people than anyone I have ever known. You be the judge: Do you think that all the hurting, heartaches and loneliness of childhood had anything to do with a heart full of compassion. Please listen again: Suffering will make us or break us. It breaks multitudes. That depends on attitude. Let us never forget the name of God's school and where it is located: The University of Affliction in the Valley of Sorrows. "Tribulation worketh patience" (Romans 5:3). That word "patience" in the Bible means steadfastness – sticking in there, strength to stand! And to stand against evil winds. The apostle said, "We glory in tribulation." You and I have not reached the heights upon which he was standing, but someday, by God's grace, we'll be there.

Jesus learned from the things which He suffered. May you and I learn from the hard knocks, and learn to see the rainbow over the clouds of storm. May we learn from the little quail as he struggles to be born, from the little lonely girl crying herself to sleep at night far away from home. And above all, may we learn from out loving Savior who "learned from the things which He suffered" (Hebrews 5:8).

Life begins with a struggle as the little babe gasps for its first breath and starts crying. It ends with a struggle as we gasp for the last breath and try to get one more. But, thanks be unto God, there is much sunshine along the way. "In that hour Jesus rejoiced." He often said, "Peace be unto you." And it is sweetly written, "God hath anointed Him with the oil of gladness above His fellows." The prophet said, "Neither be you sorryful for the joy of the Lord is your strength" (Nehemiah 8:10).

THE BIG SHIP

Sam Jones' father was a Methodist pastor. Sam was a lawyer, then a drunk. His dad died with a prayer and a broken heart over his dear son. Our gracious God saw the tears and heard the prayers of the dear man, and reached down and lifted Sam out of the jug, and put him in the pulpit as a mighty preacher.

Sam said that as a boy he lived in Florida by the sea. One morning after a bad storm, to the boy's delight, there was a big ship stranded on the shore in the sand. Not a person on or near it.

Sam fixed a way to get in and out of it, and it made the greatest playhouse any boy ever had. High tides would come, the old ship would reel and rock. Sam would jump and shout, "Come on, old ship! Go out to sea!" But the old ship remained stuck fast in the sand. The winter came, then the spring with its high tides. The full moon of spring pulled the tide way up, and the great ship rocked as if trying to free itself to sail the great ocean again. The boy, Sam, jumped for joy, clapped his hands and shouted, "Come on, old ship! You can do it, you can sail again! You were made for the big ocean. Come on!"

The old ship seemed to almost make it. It wobbled and rocked and struggled as the waters and waves rolled. But the high tide of spring went by, and there was the old ship, high and dry in the summer sun.

One morning Sam looked out and his dear old ship had fallen into a thousand pieces! Sam stood and looked at the sad sight: "Old ship, why did you end like this? You were made for the great ocean. Now it's too late!

Sam said, and I say: Many people are like the old ship – stuck in the sands. Whether it be the sands of sin, or just sand, and destined to fall, just like the old ship! The gospel comes, the high tide when the Spirit of god is calling, but there you remain – stuck! Oh, my brother; oh, my sister – you were not made to finish your life like that! While the high tide of God's call comes, like now: Step out and put your hand in the hand that hung on Calvary. The ocean of God's love is rolling like the tide, come to God now! You were given this chance. Don't let it slip by!

66

DON'T WORRY, BE HAPPY

Abraham Lincoln said, "I have noticed that most people are about as happy as they make up their minds to be." I recently mentioned a worrisome matter to my wife. She said, "Let's don't worry about that. Let's get us something else to worry about."

John Wesley remarked, "I would no more worry than I would curse and swear." It is said that his wife was very difficult to live with. Of course, that means that his home life was such that he could have worried a great deal. Yet, the great man did not worry. After he was past 80, he would ride a horse more than 50 miles to a preaching appointment. It seems that the guy who has overcome worry has tapped into God's best blessings.

The Apostle Paul, with his awful thorn in the flesh and writing from a jail cell, said, "Let nothing be worrying you." The King James puts it, "Be careful for nothing." That is, do not be burdened down with care.

It's a pity that God's people do not have a Biblical mindset. The great book says, "Godliness with contentment is great gain." And "Having food and clothing, let us therewith be contended." I think the writer assumes one has a shelter to sleep under.

An article in the Christian Index started me thinking about doing all my worrying one day a month. Just set that day aside and save up all my worrying for that day. And as I practiced this, I would probably find that, in retrospect, most of my troubles had already cleared up. Too, the few left could not be changed by worry. Also, as my worry day drew near, God was blessing me abundantly. I needed to spend more time giving thanks. No time to worry. Thank God.

By the way, you don't have to wait for circumstances to become ideal to stop worrying. In a South Carolina church, our baptistery was metal and needed much repair by a welder. Our men knew the county officials so they got prison labor to do it. The welder drove a pick up to the church each day. My study was in the church, so we became great friends. Both the guys were trustees. That means they had a lot of liberty, and it took them many days. They didn't hurry.

My wife thinks I can do anything. She wanted me to cut some holes in a metal flowerpot so the flowers could come out of the sides as well as the top. I told her to get the prisoner to do it with his blowtorch. "He's a nice guy," I assured her. She approached him, "Mr. Chalker, do you think you'll have the time," she said, almost pleadingly. He replied nonchalantly, "Lady, I reckon I got time. They tell me I got 25 years." He ended up in prison by trying to kill his wife's lover. But the wrong guy was under the steering wheel, and he killed the wrong fellow!

Strange: He seemed to be a very happy man, and he told me that he was never happy until he "Got on the chain gang." (They had those very words, "chain gang" on their mailbox). He said, "All my life I was drinking and getting into trouble. Now, he said, "I've been converted, and I'm happy for the first time in my life." There he was with 25 years in that South Carolina Chain Gang and whistling a happy tune. Happier than most of our church members. That should teach us something. It's like honest Abe said, "People are about as happy as they make up their minds to be."

If you would find lasting happiness, reach out your hand by faith, and clasp the hand that hung on Calvary! It was He who said, "Come unto me and I will give you rest."

A PUFF OF SMOKE

Attending my little home town's centennial celebration, I saw and became reacquainted with Roman Brown, whom I had not seen in a lifetime, and had completely forgotten that he was in the world. He delighted in telling the only thing he remembered about me. And, although I regretted that it happened, I delighted equally in hearing it, especially since his eyes gleamed so as he seemed to relive the hour.

He said, "We were lined up to march into the school house, and Mrs. Carr, the principal, was standing in front of us on the elevated porch platform. I noticed that she seemed to be looking off in the distance," Roman said, "and I looked that way, and saw a puff of smoke come from behind a tree." I looked back at Mrs. Carr. She was still looking, so I looked back, and your head came slowly from behind that tree. Mrs. Carr yelled, "Thero! Come out from behind that tree and get in line." You came out alright, Roman remembered gleefully, "but you walked in the other direction, with that cigarette in your mouth."

After a lifetime of years had passed by, that's the ONE THING my boyhood friend remembered about me! And you know what? Roman Brown was no different from the rest of us. We are all like that. That's part of our "fallen nature". We remember the bad about people, even about our friends, far more than we do the good. It's human nature! And we find ways of never letting bad things die. Even we preachers are that way, and even in our sermons! But God is not like that by His children! We have a wonderful God!

For instance, I have heard several sermons about the Old Testament character named Lot. All through all of these sermons, not one good word have I EVER heard a preacher say about Lot! How different from God. Many hundreds of years later, God mentions Lot in the New Testament, and guess what He calls him? "THAT RIGHTEOUS MAN!" And God tells us that Lot's "righteous soul" was grieved by the evil around him (II Peter 2:8).

It is even much better than wonderful that our God has a way of forgetting the sins of His people! He says, "I will remember your iniquities no more." God has a way of seeing the good in His children. Let us Christians follow God's example, and see the good in one another. Even the boy puffing the cigarette may have had SOMETHING good about him?! At least God loved him.

THE SUNNY SIDE

Certain scriptures and scriptural statements we need to forever keep repeating, and some truths we pick up along life's way are like that. The Loma Linda study revealed that after people laugh for thirty minutes their red blood cells are up twenty percent. The Bible statement, "A merry heart does good like a medicine." And the added statement, "But a broken spirit drieth up the bones". (Pro. 17:22).

And never forget God's repeated instructions to Joshua as this man started standing in Moses' stead: In a nutshell it was, "Be strong and of good courage." And God repeated it to him four or five times. Awesome was the weight bearing down on him. "Every-day strength" would not do. It had to be "Sunday-go-to-meeting" strength! Only God could give it.

But God speaks to Joshua as if he can be strong by *resolving to do so*. And it is true that man's strength is at its best when he makes up his mind to be strong. An athlete can play his best game when he enters the game with his mind made up to play his best game. When a prize fighter enters the ring this way, people say, "He came to fight!" That's the way God wills for us to enter *each day*, and to *go through life!*

Part of this needed strength comes by looking on the sunny side. Gazing into the darkness, listening to the thunder, can be frightful and discouraging. It is a champion at bringing on depression, and if continued, it leads to the valley of ruin.

A merry heart is a medicine from God. As in the Loma Linda case, it strengthens the immune system and gives strength, joy and courage to the heart. Let us "lift up our eyes to the hills whence cometh our help. Our help cometh from the Lord, who made heaven and earth" (Ps. 121:1-).

However, our strength comes mostly by walking with Him who *is* strong. God is the source of our strength. Never forget the statement: "For *He (God) is your life* and the length of your days" (Deu. 30:20). The Jewish leaders of the New Testament days saw the power and strength of Jesus' disciples and they "Took notice that they had been with Jesus!" Yes, yes, He is eternal, and tied to Him, we can't even die! The sunny side and the shining face of our God is our medicine and our life! And it's our pillow when we come to die. We'll hold His hand, and He will hold ours, and *even*

Death will be turned into life!

GOD TALKS TO US IN THE BIBLE
GOD'S WORD, DAVID'S TONGUE

How assuring that the Bible claims to be the Word of God. Such statements as: "The Lord spoke, the Lord said, and God said, the word of the Lord came" – in hundreds of places we find such statements.

Look at these statements about how David lived his life: These sweet words from the Lord about David: "David who kept my commandments and followed me with ALL his heart, to do ONLY that which was right in mine eyes." (I Kings 14:8). Then, as if that's not enough, listen to God again: "Because David did that, which was right in the eyes of the Lord and turned not aside from anything that He commanded him all the days of his life, save only in the matter of Uriah the Hittite" (I Kings 15:5).

It was God's word and David's tongue. We could say, God was doing the speaking and David was doing the talking. It was both God and man!

In the New Testament, Acts 1:16, is an interesting reference to David on this same subject: "This Scripture must need have been fulfilled, which the Holy Ghost spoke by the mouth of David." See, it was both David's mouth and the blessed Holy Spirit doing the talking.

It was like the teacher and the little child's first writing. The child's hand was guiding the pencil and over that little hand was a larger hand and far more accurate, that of the wise teacher guiding the little hand. When Jesus was here, although they only had the Old Testament, He often made reference to the Holy Scriptures. And it was always as if they could be counted on as trustworthy and accurate. And, remember, Jesus was the BLESSED SON OF GOD! Although the Bible is an old book, it is a book that never grows old! "Thy word is a lamp to my feet and a light to my path" (Psalms 119:105). We are pilgrims and strangers here and this book shows us the way home. It is this book that guides our feet toward and to Heaven's Shining Shores.

A MIGHTY KING
DANIEL, CHAPTER FOUR

In a dream this mighty king saw a tree that reached unto heaven and its shade and branches covered the whole earth! The whole human race and the beasts of the field and forest benefited by this great tree, eating of its fruit and basking in its shade. Then the tree was cut down and only its stump and its roots remained.

When all others failed, Daniel was called to interpret, and when Daniel saw the great meaning of it all, he sat in astonishment for one hour and the king sought to console him. Daniel exclaimed: "Oh, My Dear Sir, the dream is to the pleasure of your enemies! The tree, O King, is YOU and you are going to be cut down and driven from your throne and from the people until you realize that there is a God in heaven who rules above the kings, and you will eat with the animals of the fields and forest, with the beast there, until you come to bow your knees before God."

Then Daniel, with his big heart, humbly urged the great king to straighten up and fly right. But this great king, like so many of the rest of us, like the ox headed for the slaughter, continued his evil ways. And his sins did to him what the armies of the world could not do! He lived for seven long years in the fields and forest and ate the wild beasts' food.

Loneliness and rejection can overcome and kill the strongest of men. As the years went by, he became broken in body, mind and soul. Evidently this was a complete mental breakdown and even more. Friendless, hopeless, a broken man, he lived from day-to-day, as the years passed. King Nebuchadnezzer was a mighty strong man, but the hell and horror of such a life is just too much! It is the wages of sin, which is death. He must have died a thousand deaths!

However, our God is merciful and He hung a little light in the sky for this dear man, whom God had not forgotten. A little light like that of a wee dim candle in the dark and far away. And this, once a great man, started his stumbling steps in that direction. God helped him, and in his own words: "I lifted up mine eyes to Heaven and mine understanding returned!"

God had great mercy on the dear man and gave him back, (LISTEN): His mind, his health, his throne, his friends! All because he "lifted up his eyes to heaven!"

LESSONS TO BE LEARNED HERE:

1. GOD PUTS KINGS ON THE THRONE AND HE TAKES THEM DOWN.

    * This is taught repeatedly in the Scriptures.

2. SIN WILL BRING ANYONE DOWN:

    * A heathen saying with much truth implied: "The mills of the gods grind slow, but exceedingly find."

3. REPENTANCE WORKS WONDERS WITH GOD:

    * Learning our lessons and turning our feet, and hearts is a must.

    * The Good Book says: "God commands all men everywhere to repent.

    * Repentance is a change of mind and such a change of mind that it turns the feet into the proper path.

4. AFTER ALL THIS, GOD WORKED WONDERS FOR THIS MAN:

    * He was not a Jew, not of Abraham's seed, yet God's hand reached far into the darkness of heathendom an did wonders for him.

5. IT WAS WHEN HE "LIFTED UP HIS EYES TO HEAVEN" THAT GOD'S HEART OF LOVE WAS POURED UPON HIM.

50th Anniversary

74

A GREAT TREE

Sometimes I think there is more in this world that I don't understand, than that I do. I stood and studied a tall pecan tree, which had lost most of its leaves. Much fruit could be clearly seen, even up in its tall top. I thought: That tree took nutrients – vitamins and minerals – from in the ground, the air and the sunlight, and had the ability to harvest all that, bring it together and make good food out of it! And it put the same mixture into every one of those pecans! It must have a lot of measuring spoons. Man with all of his learning cannot do that.

We people are like the old mule. He watched the honeybee go into the blossom after blossom around his feet. Finally, the old mule asked, "Just what are you doing?" "I'm gathering honey to take to the hive," the little bee answered. "Well, where are you getting it?" "Out of these blossoms, don't you see me?" "Huh," replied the old mule, "You can't fool me, they ain't no honey there; I've eaten a million of them."

Well, "they ain't none there" for the old mule, and they ain't none for you and me. But plenty for the little bee. See? Everywhere we look, we see a mystery.

That pecan tree not only gets its nutrients and taste from where "they ain't none," it forms each piece into a beautiful pattern, puts a light brown coat on each and tucks each securely into a little strong box. And it <u>makes </u>the box, then, it locks the door. It gives each nut, not only its delicious taste and nutrients, making it good for birds and beasts and you and me, but also the ability to, when put back in the ground, <u>make itself into another giant tree just like its mama!</u> A series of miracles that we take for granted.

Mysteries everywhere! The Bible could not have spoken a truer word than, "Now, we see through a glass darkly." We accept millions of things by faith. Likewise, in the spiritual realm, we walk by faith and not by sight, just as the Bible says.

Since we do our earthly, natural lives by faith, let us live our spiritual lives the same way. Jesus said of God and man, "Blessed are they who believe and have not seen." Little faith, exercised, will take us to Heaven; big faith will bring Heaven to us.

HARDSHIPS –
THEY MAKE OR BREAK US

It seems that God has chosen hardships and suffering as a part of our training. The Bible says, "Let them that suffer ACCORDING TO THE WILL OF GOD…" (1 Peter 4:19). This surely tells us that it is the WILL OF GOD that we suffer at times. When God selected Saul to be the great apostle Paul, God said, "I will show him how great things he must suffer for my name's sake" (Acts 9:16). He was called to a life of suffering. Sure, there was much sunshine, and joy of the Holy Spirit. But there was the suffering side.

Let us not raise our children with the idea that they will get through this life with nothing but silver spoons and ice cream in their mouths. If we do, likely the sufferings they encounter will ruin them. Sufferings make and sufferings break. Our attitude has much to do with the outcome.

We need to know, yes even in youth, that suffering is a part of real life. Romans 5:3 says, "We glory in tribulations, knowing that tribulation worketh patience." "Patience" here means "steadfastness", sticking in there. We Christians are taught to stick with God by the deep waters we go through!!

Long ago, near the tail end of the World Wide Great Depression, Leonard Harbin and his young wife, Estelle, moved from the countryside to Augusta, Ga. Augusta in those days was one of the starvation capitals of America.

After many disappointing days, Leonard said, "Estelle, let's go to Columbus, Ga., I can get a job there." Soon they had their little bit of duds packed and were on a bus, with their pockets empty and Estelle's arms filled with her baby boy. No money, no job, no promise; just poverty!

But God works in mysterious ways, His wonders to perform. He plants His feet upon the sea, He rides upon the storm!

As that bus rolled over non-paved roads, rains fell in torrents. Finally, the old lizzy came to a stop. The driver needed to get out

76

into the mud. Leonard Harbin was an outgoing person, always wanting to help anyone, and he had on boots. He said, "Mr. Driver, put on my boots if you are going to get out in that mud." Off and on the boots came and went, and soon the bus was rolling again. The driver insisted that Leonard accept two dollars for the use of the boots. As Leonard pocketed those two dollars, he looked at the driver's shoulders to see if he had any wings, for he knew that it was the Lord who sent those two precious bucks to one whose family was so desperately in need.

Arriving in Columbus and walking down a street as night was falling, there was a sign, "ROOM FOR RENT". They walked up and knocked on the door. "Lady," Leonard dared to say, "I've just come to this town. This is my family. I don't have a job, but I'm going to get one. We need a room to live in. Would you rent me this room on a credit? I'm broke."

The kindhearted lady looked into the little baby boy's face, and into the face of the innocent-looking mother. She thought she heard a tone of honesty in Leonard's voice. And like the princess looking into the face of little Moses in the Nile, her heart was moved. There was only one answer she had the strength to give.

Before retiring for the night, this tired couple with their baby knelt by the bed to say their prayers. They told God how broke their pockets were and how bleeding their hearts were. They thanked Him for the room and bed and for the dear lady who had graciously afforded it for them, and they asked Him to help Leonard to get a job.

Estelle told me later that the dear lady was listening through a crack in the door as the two strangers in her home prayed. The Good Samaritan was up early the next morning and at the grocery for the three precious people God had sent her way. Then as they prayed, sang and ate together at the good lady's table, the two newcomers wondered if this was not the same angels whom God sent to bake the cake for Elijah.

Leonard got a job making eight dollars a week and they enjoyed living in that one room with the angel whom God had sent their way, rather to whom God had sent them.

77

When we think of our Great and dear God and the path that we have traveled, so many of us like to sing, "Great is thy faithfulness….. All I have needed thy hand hath provided." And I seem to hear Lazarus who lay at the rich man's gate shout, "AMEN!"

THE WEB OF WONDERS

The first twenty-seven years of this writer's life were spent in the fields and forest. Many times in God's great wilderness I would come upon a huge spider web, larger than double doors. I sometimes stood and looked at the big web with wonder, built with such amazing ability, knowledge and wisdom – such uniformity, and done overnight!

Our architects need twelve years of schooling, plus college, special courses, then on-the-job training. But this little lady builds her houses – no training at all, builds it overnight. An amazing network of architecture, far beyond anything I have ever seen!

It is not only a home to live, air-conditioned, swinging in the breeze, it actually earns a livelihood for the builder! She does not have to work a job. Her house affords her food. Imagine starting with nothing, no material, no tools, and building your house in one night. And when finished, you don't owe the bank a penny. In addition to being a miracle, the house brings home the bacon.

No training at all. And listen to this: She eats bugs and she has a manufacturing plant on the inside of her that turns these bugs into building material. It's beyond me. All this, and she is smaller than my thumb!

A verse in the Bible: "Now we see through a glass darkly." That is, we understand little. Almost everywhere we look there's something we don't understand. Jesus said to Nicodemus, "I've told you earthly things and you don't understand that, if I were to tell you heavenly things, things about Heaven, how could you get any of it? You don't understand things that happen right before your eyes."

In God's great world, we are not required to understand but to trust. In the Old Testament the word "faith" is used only twice. It' word for faith is "trust." "Trust in the Lord with all your heart, and lean not unto thine own understanding. In all your ways acknowledge Him, and He shall direct your paths." (Proverbs 3:5-6)

HOPE

A certain true story of a beautiful and devoted dog is powerfully impressive about the importance of hope to all of us. Life hangs on hope. This Chinese Chow was young and strong, had lived only in a palace and known nothing but love and kindness, petting and patting. The family went on a very long vacation. The poor dog was in a cage where the vet and others were all too busy. The poor dog. How could he know they were ever coming back, or why they forsook him?

Each day and night was so very long! He finally lost hope. When they eventually came to pick him up, they found that he had died a few hours before they arrived. Caused by a heart attack and brought on by grief. So it is when hope goes with both man and beast.

In the Bible and out of the Bible, "hope" is a word of wonders. When God would give us our most precious possessions, he handed us only three: Faith, Hope and Love.

If I were translating the New Testament, for hope, I'd use two words: *hope-assurance.* That would give this word the strength it had in New Testament days. Thus we would get the full meaning as in the New Testament. For this word HOPE, is a mighty word in the Bible. Even Jesus, God's dear Son, is called "Our Hope" in First Timothy. And in connection with His second coming. He is: "OUR BLESSED HOPE!" When God would give us the best in life, He gave us three things" *Faith, Hope and Love.*

As Christians, we make a tragic mistake when we fix our hope too tightly on anything in this life or world. It is all so vanishing. Even the most successful marriages and families break up, yes, everyone. The marriage comes to an end by the side of a sad grave and the family around many graves watered with tears. Even our health will fade every time and earthly life itself will soon end.

The Book tells us that God has given us both His word and His oath "that we might have a strong consolation," a strong assurance, a strong hope-assurance.

"Which hope we have as anchor of the soul, both sure and steadfast" (See Heb. 6:16-19). If we fix our hope too tight on earthly things, our hope tends to weaken in Heavenly things. This makes disappointments. Jesus taught this, "Lay not up for yourself treasures on earth, but lay up treasures in Heaven" (Mt. 6:19—). We won't always have our homes, our families, our health, or any earthly thing. But we will always have God. "For He is your life," the Book says. We will have Him and He will have us forever.

TO KEEP YOUR HOPE BURNING BRIGHT, KEEP YOUR FAITH IN THE LIGHT.

THE SHEPHERD, THE SHEEP, AND THE SHEEPDOGS

Shepherds have learned that sheep dogs are better shepherds than shotguns when it comes to protecting the sheep. And they are learning to raise the little puppies and lambs all mixed in with the big dogs and sheep. THAT WAY, they all accept each other much better, and seem to hardly know, or care, about the difference.

But time and experience have taught the shepherds that after all their training, and with the shepherd even living with the sheep and the dogs night and day, yet the man is still a man, the dog a dog, and the sheep are still sheep.

It all works beautifully, and it is amazing – the dog's great wisdom and how he achieves in doing his duty, herding and protecting the sheep.

Yet, it is <u>by no means unknown for the faithful dog to turn and kill the very sheep he is living to protect,</u> even to kill a little lamb. One shepherd put it: "There's something in these dogs – something in him and in the elements of the night, the dog's ancestry, the wind and the wilds, and there's something within him, and it's always there – he seems changed into a different dog."

81

LISTEN: All that is not just dogs. We people are like that too! Thank God, we are often and much like the faithful dog. Then there is danger that something rise up within us and we become like the unfaithful dog. Jesus knew this much better than we know it, and that's why He cautioned us: "The spirit indeed is willing, but the flesh is weak." You're mighty right it's weak, and you better know it!

"Flesh" there means something in our nature that pulls us down and toward sin and the wild, the way people go who know not God. That "something" has been in our ancestry since Adam. It's in every one of us. It accounts for all the wars, crime and callousness. It pulls people away from God and into sin and to Satan. Indeed, it caused man to crucify his Maker! Let us learn the lesson from the dogs!

However, there's something else in the faithful dogs, something that pulls him back to the flock, to faithfulness and duty, to love for his master. And so it is in us, especially in God's children. People who know and love God can never find heart fulfillment in the wilds of the world, as we once did. With the shepherd and the sheep the faithful dog finds fulfillment for his heart's desire. Oh may you and I forever hear the call of our Master and find loving care in His wonderful fold.

THE LITTLE KITTY CAT

Let's think about him. A friend of mine told me about a friend of his, and the little kitty cat. They were big buddies. When the man came home from work each day, the little kitty would meet him and greet him. Then, when the tired man lay down to rest his weary bones, the little kitty would come and lie with his soft head on the man's shoulder. They were real chums.

Then a baby was born into the family, and the little newborn quickly became allergic to the little kitty. This brought a real problem to both the man and the kitty. The doctor said the kitty must go. My! What problems we can have in this world of weal and woe!

Almost in shock, the man took the little kitty in his arms. Hugged him up close and said, "Little Kitty, you have to leave here, leave your home, and me. We're going to miss each other, and you won't understand. He hugged his little furry friend close, and said, "I wish I could be a kitty for just five minutes, so I could talk your language and tell you about it, and tell you how much I love you, and hate to see you go. Maybe you would understand that it just has to be."

That so well illustrates another far greater truth. God Almighty wanted us to understand more about Himself and His sweet love for us. So He said within Himself, "I'll become a person, like them. I'll go down and walk and talk with them, and love them. I'll teach them and do many good things for them. I'll lift their loads and carry their burdens. I'll walk in their moccasins."

So, God left His home in Heaven and came and was one with us. His name was Jesus. He lifted our loads and talked our language. He even took our sins and bore them on the cross until God said, "It is enough. It is finished."

In the Bible, John said, "Our eyes have seen and our hands have handled of the Word of Life." When Jesus was walking around on this earth, Philip said something like, "Lord, you've healed the sick and raised the dead. Now just do one other thing and that will be enough. Stand our Heavenly Father down here and let us look Him over." And Jesus' answer was very revealing: "Philip, have I been so long with you and you have not seen me. He that hath seen me hath seen the Father" (John 14:8,9).

The Book says that "God was in Christ reconciling the world unto Himself." To reconcile means bring back. The Bible pictures the whole world with its back on God, going its sinful and wild way away from God, and Jesus came to turn us around and bring us back to God. Have you been brought back?

THE LITTLE MONKEY

I am told that in the South Sea islands, the natives have a nifty way of catching monkeys, which they eat. They build a cage and put a coconut in it. The monkey reaches his hand in and gets the coconut. He will not turn loose and he can't get his hand out with the coconut in it.

Now, if I could visit those islands and talk monkey talk, I would say, "Little monkey, I have been watching you play around here, and I like you. Listen, little monkey, these natives are coming. They are going to kill, boil and eat you. Run, little monkey, run! Let go and run fast!"

But he's got such a hold on that coconut, and that coconut has such a hold on him - it seems that he just can't turn loose. So they come and kill, and boil, and eat him. He has the great pleasure of dying with the coconut in his hand. How foolish is the monkey!

You know what: There are many monkeys in America just like that. Some of these American monkeys are presidents of banks and universities, and some are carpenters and clerks. They have such a hold on the world, or some special evil - and the world has such a hold on them - they never turn loose. The grim reaper comes and cuts them down, and drags them to destruction, even to Hell!

A rich young ruler came to Jesus. He had his hand in the cage. He asked, "Master, how can I be free and have eternal life?" Jesus said, "Turn it all loose. Give it all up. Come, take up the cross and follow me." (See Luke 18:18-)

Giving up the world and the ways of the world is a part of being converted. Jesus said, "Except you to be converted, you shall in no wise enter." Give it up, my brother, give it up, else you will be as foolish as the monkey.

ETERNITY

As I listen to people speak of eternity, I wonder how much thought has been given to this all-important subject. The main things folks say here is to speak of "spending eternity." Why, you can't <u>spend</u> eternity. When you spend something it is gone, whether it be a day or a dollar. And eternity is never gone. You don't spend it.

As a farm boy in the long past, where we labored and laughed, when I was eleven, my dad stuck me in the field with a mule. I had to keep him going and keep up with him. And that went on for thirteen years! When you look at the north end of a south-bound mule for thirteen years, as the guy said, "You done done something! You done went and got yo' self a good education!" And on Saturdays, after a hard week's work, my dear old Dad would give me a quarter. I could go to town that afternoon and "spread it on."

I'd go in Van Moad's little dinky store and play the slot machine. Those oranges and cherries would turn beautifully, and generally, I'd get nothing. And if it gave me a few nickels, I'd put them right back. You are whipped before you start with those one-armed bandits. If I had any left, I'd buy some candy. Of course, I'd go home broke. Go to town rich, with a quarter, then go home bankrupt. I had spent it all! When you spend it, it's gone.

Well, you can't spend eternity. It's never gone!

And people talk about "all" of eternity. There's no such thing as **all** of eternity. None of us can EVEN THINK of the end of it, for there is no end!

What a glorious thought this is! This truth that God gives us in the Bible, and also gives by His Great Spirit directly into our hearts and minds. Just the thought that when we Christians die, or when Jesus comes, He will take us into His loving arms to live eternally in the land that is fairer than day! A land where the sun never sets and all tears are wiped away.

The unbeliever says, "You're just dreaming." If I'm dreaming, let me sleep on. It's the sweetest dream I ever had! But the fact is, God is real, God is true! His home will be our home. How great it is to love Jesus and be one of his followers. Although many of us may not be the best of His followers, it's still sweet to be one. He already died on the cross for us, and now He lives to take us to Heaven. You can't beat a Savior like that!

To contact the author please write or call
Mr. & Mrs. T.W. Snider at:
835 Maple Drive
Riverdale, Ga 30274
770-477-1622